FADO
& OTHER
STORIES

WINNER OF THE DRUE HEINZ LITERATURE PRIZE 1997

KATHERINE VAZ

FADO

& OTHER STORIES

UNIVERSITY OF PITTSBURGH PRESS

Published by the

University of Pittsburgh Press,

Pittsburgh, Pa. 15261

Copyright © 1997, Katherine Vaz

Manufactured in the United States of America

Printed on acid-free paper

10   9   8   7   6   5   4   3   2   1

Library of Congress

Cataloging-in-Publication Data

Vaz, Katherine.

Fado & other stories / Katherine Vaz.

p. cm.

"The Drue Heinz literature prize."

ISBN 0-8229-4051-5 (alk. paper)

I. Title. II. Title: Fado and other stories.

PS3572.A97F34   1997   97-4822

813'.54—dc21   CIP

A CIP catalog record for this book is
available from the British Library.

For my mother,

Elizabeth Sullivan Vaz,

whose love of stories is at

the center of my history,

and for my father,

August Mark Vaz,

whose love of history regarding

his Azorean heritage has led me

to so many magical stories

Quem fez os homens e deu vida aos lobos?

Santa Teresa em místicos arroubos?

Os monstros? E os profetas? E o luar?

[Who made men and gave life to the wolves?

To Saint Teresa in her mystical raptures?

To monsters? And to the prophets? And to the moonlight?]

—Florbela Espanca, from the sonnet "?"

CONTENTS

FADO
& OTHER
STORIES

ORIGINAL SIN

One day without provocation my brother hit me with a shovel. That it came as a dark flash from nowhere stunned me as much as the blow, and after the doctor stitched up my head, he peered into my eyes to make certain I had not gone too far into another world. When my parents asked my brother why he had struck me, he looked without expression at them. "Because I've never seen Miranda cry," he finally said, as bewildered as anybody. From that day I have never doubted the existence of original sin. Nothing has since grown on my head where the shovel landed.

The artichoke was king in Castroville. We sold them, ate them, and under the guidance of Father Armando Ortigão stuck their thorns into our fingers for penance. Actually, until we died we could chew raw onions and traipse the perimeters of our farms on our knees, and it would still not wash clean the stain of what man was. Father Ortigão drew a heart on the chalkboard to explain: At first glance it looks blank and pure, until we realize that it must take its shape against a black background if it is to exist.

In fifth grade I discovered sorrow and longing. Merely touching the new hair around my labia set off a grotesque aching. I developed a fever for riding horses, I did unspeakable things to dolls. I figured, this being a finite world, that after coming a certain number of times I could be done forever with depravity, but when this did not appear to be happening I had terrible visions of myself as an unsated old woman, still sliding down banisters, still burning. Perhaps original sin was another name for desire.

Because we could not build snowmen in Castroville, we made men and babies out of mud. We gave them dry straw hair and invited them to our tea parties, where we served sugar water infused with mint leaves that were white from crop dusting. When the men dried and cracked in the sun, we mixed up new ones. All over the inner valley in our part of north central California, we could uncover the dust of the broken. Ants swarmed over shattered arms and coal eyes.

The Portuguese women left *figuras de cera* for God where the sun could anoint the glints of melting wax with prism rainbows that would catch His eye. During a flu epidemic, we tripped over puddles of wax stomachs in the fields. Behind the church was the favorite spot for wax hearts. If the heart melted and the patient lived, God had accepted the offering and spared the man. If the heart melted and the patient died, it was a personal sign that God was calling him home to the great pool of souls.

The Church always won.

When Almir Cruz got drunk and shot off one of his testicles, the girls searched high and low, past the softening eyes, legs, and livestock *de cera* of petitioners, hoping to discover his wax balls. I stayed out late with a flashlight, desperately wanting to find Almir.

This desire to make a treasure hunt out of the sad prayers and wants of others ended when my father and brother died in a car wreck, in the stretch where we converged with outsiders. The road, like most of the ones in California, always smelled like blood. Tourists pulled on and off the highway so fast, stopping to buy cheap artichokes, that our lives were always hemmed in by fearsome machines. Witnesses called the accident a blinding flash, too fast to anticipate. Within a year my mother took to her bed with lung cancer. She breathed clean air and did not smoke, so I knew she was dying for love.

My aunt helped me make wax lungs, complete with realistic veins. They looked like butterfly wings when we put them in the sun.

Father Ortigão would come to the house, urging my mother to make her peace with the world.

Tia Ofélia would come to the house, urging me to melt on her lap in the slump of the grieving child.

My father once explained to me the solitude of the Portuguese. We would rather go out to sea alone in a small boat than fish together on a big one. The Mexicans and Italians in Castroville had a much better grasp on the strength behind the collective haul. We clamored instead after distance, *put your back to me and let us pace apart.* We bought land for power but mostly for isolation.

Solitude breeds two things: lust and a need to scour. One of my neighbors was sleeping with both the wife and daughter of a nearby farm, except on Sundays, when he undertook the impossible job of trying to clean a stable so thoroughly that it would never need cleaning again.

Father Armando Ortigão patted my mother's hand and assured her that it was completely within her power to care for me, if she would simply help him provide. "Even the dying can perform good works," he said.

Portuguese boasts succinct words for every nuance of ardor and purification.

Ansiar: to burn for, and to be a source of anxiety to. No one word in English so clearly states that love can be such a pestering, unattainable, unquenchable blind side as to instill fear in another's heart.

Esfregar, limpar, arear: to scrub, to clean, to scour with sand.

How many ways can solitary people restate the wish to tidy their lives? Eyes evolved in isolation see disorder in the smallest corners and tucks.

Despite so many dark and light words, there were none that covered how I longed for a restorative for my mother as I watched her skin sink. Nor could I think how to blot away my silence and the poison that swarmed in the room when Father Ortigão held up, as if in consecration, the deed to my dead father's land.

Before she died, my mother agreed that she should make her life a clean slate. While I stood by, Father Ortigão helped her sign the deed over to the Church. He promised it would slash her Purgatory time down to only the laundering away of original sin, a spate in the fire from which only martyrs were exempt. He wished he could do more, but some things, he told her with a smile, were beyond his grasp.

An oily feast marked my official ushering into the care of Tia Ofélia. She was an aging woman who would never dream of accepting money from a priest, even if the land on which he planned to build a winery had once belonged to my family, even if he had offered.

She was grateful that Father Ortigão had relieved her and me of trying to enter heaven with the weight of earthly property pulling us down near the rich man who had denied his table leavings to Lazarus the beggar. The rich man had ended up in hell, screaming for a drop of water. That story always rang false in my ears. If the afterlife was all forgiveness and peace, why did Moses allow Lazarus, when safely in heaven, to deny the burning creature's request?

Father Ortigão had promised my mother that I would have food and a roof over my head, but he did not mention that Tia Ofélia and not the land would be my delivering angel.

Crabs and artichokes were served at my adoption banquet. Men cracked the briny shells and legs with mallets to get to the soft ocean taste. They pulled leaves off the artichokes, and cleared aside the choke to unearth the roots. Knives sliced through the vibrissae and the purple tissues that fluttered out from the hearts like butterflies. The table was heaped with discards. Father Ortigão would occasionally lift his head from his feasting, his face shining with grease.

I remembered a night when I stumbled across Almir Cruz in a field with Angela Figueira, before his accident. He had peeled away the layers of clothing protecting her, snapped open her legs, and was about to dive for her tender flesh.

I ran away then from fear, and I ran from the table now because this time the violation was against me.

My dear Tia Ofélia died the same day as the groundbreaking for the new Transfiguration School gym. For a long time I slept ten hours a night, my arms around a pillow, but when the Castroville Christian Winery increased its admission to one dollar a person and charged the tour buses five to park, I donned a spotless white uniform and headed over to the rectory. Father Ortigão had grown silver-haired and much beloved by the parishioners. It was widely noted that even the money he had so generously given me after the sale of my parents' house, razed to clear a spot for wine cellar expansion, had failed to attract a man to me. Naturally I smiled at this kind of talk.

I persuaded him that with the turmoil surrounding the new buildings, he needed a housekeeper. With Tia Ofélia gone, I had no one left in the world. Didn't he remember how my mother had trusted him to take care of me?

To teach Father Ortigão to dive, I would toss a gold hoop into the shallows of the lake. In water I had license to put my arms around him, to hoist him up for air. I pressed my breasts against his back, my nose against his neck, and pulled. I could touch his shoulders and run my bare foot against his knees to relax him for the plunge.

Soon after the summer heat drove me from a one-piece to a two-piece suit, he declared our swimming lessons over. I scolded him for giving up before the deed was done. Now that he was getting set to build a Transfiguration pool, how would it look when everyone found out that he sank like a stone? What was he afraid of? Like every good priest, he was supposed to think of water as baptism, renewal, the beginning of a new life.

"You win, Miranda," he said.

When I forgot to bring a towel or change of clothes, I would undress back at the rectory while dripping into some of his long white shirts. I would stretch my bikini out to dry on the veranda.

Swimming gave him an appetite for charred meat, potatoes, mayonnaise, strawberry pies, rum, cabernet sauvignon. I poured him different wines with each meal, insisting that as driving force behind the Castroville Christian Winery he must sample what he had all along been giving to others.

I kept the rectory immaculate. One would not think a man alone could do so much damage, but I managed to find plenty to clean. I sponged spiders' nests out of corners, dusted light bulbs in their sockets, refilled the brandy decanter. When I aired out comforters and broke into a sweat, my blouse turned translucent in patches.

"Miranda," he said to me one day. "O my God, I can't get rid of you. Can I?"

I weakened for a moment, when I saw him as a man alone, grown thick around the middle, with liver spots on his scalp, when, with eschatological bent, I thought a brutish build should not condemn him as a brute. He blinked at dust in a light mote, and I considered that every single one of us is defenseless unto death. But not all of us dabble so freely with others defenseless *in* death, and I reminded myself that the so-called forgiving God had answered Adam's plea for mercy by forbidding automatic sanctifying grace to eons of generations after him.

When I discovered Father Ortigão working over the Castroville Christian Winery's annual tally, my nerves steeled. I pulled off my shirt and melted onto his lap in the slump of the aggrieved child.

During my affair with Father Armando Ortigão, he satisfied himself again and again, but my feelings were obviously not his concern. I preferred the arrogance of him imagining that what was making him burst was doing the same for me. I could not bend over with my scrub brush without him unleashing a torrent of frenzy from behind. He pushed my face into the couch or against a table so I could not gaze at his pent-up years coming undone. Whenever he pressed full length on me I wrapped my legs around him but even with the dig of my heels I did not exist in this embrace.

How Father Ortigão could toy with life without thinking of consequences will always astound me. *If* the entangled vines on my father's land are allowed to grow, *then* don't they yield wine? *If* all he can see is his own desire, *then* doesn't it take a baby to make him see me?

He accused me of being Eve with the apple.

I said that all I did was provide the black background against which he could shape his heart.

I had no intention of being bundled up under cover of night, the way the plagued are borne away, to wait for the Good Shepherd nuns to seize my child the second the crown split my legs and deliver it to a nice deserving couple. The home was hidden away in Napa, a place of too-visible secrets, where gospel readings and the rain drilled the bad girls clean. We would be handed buckets of pine water to keep our scandalous home pure.

Desperation made Father Ortigão shameless in his arguments about why I should commend myself to the nuns.

I told him I had commended myself to him instead. I also told half of Castroville, although one parishioner would have been sufficient for everyone, down to the workmen in the damp, musty

Christian cellar, to know within moments that acts of love and grace can be actual, if not always sanctifying.

Some nights now I look around my house, at my husband slumbering in his chair after a hard day at the dairy, and it is hard to muster quarrel with life. Old-fashioned Christmas ornaments, an avocado seed sprouting near a window, silk from the valley's corn stuck like cat hair on the furniture—merely seeing these things can trigger contentment. What I do not have is the love of my daughter, who is traveling through America with a man I have warned her is nothing but trouble. When we do speak, it is because she gets me on the phone instead of Darryl, who feels that her demands for money and her cries from the bottom of a glass are the burden of being a priest's child.

Darryl is a good and forgiving man, or he most certainly would not have taken up my cause when shame drove Father Ortigão from Castroville and my plan to reclaim my father's land backfired. The Bishop laughed at my demand, in fact, but agreed that I was entitled to a small, one-time amount to make certain that the innocent child was not punished for the sins of its parents and its Church. I told myself that although I had not won back my legacy, I had rid myself of the perpetrator of the original sin against it.

Whenever I see my daughter's photo on the mantel, I know that I am a fool. I have won nothing—aside from the man who became my rescuer from hateful stares—other than the warning that answering evil with evil ensures that it stays in the blood.

In my aloneness when Darryl falls asleep, I wonder why the only person I have brought to life is so far from my reach. The burning in me will not wash clean. I slip ice onto my tongue and into my clothes to fight the valley heat, but even many drops of water bring me no relief.

THE
BIRTH OF
WATER
STORIES

We must make love quickly; I wish the doctors were not waiting right outside the door. I draw aside the white bedsheet and under my touch, whether through familiar reflex or desire, you grow hard enough for me to lift my skirt and climb onto you. They have covered what remains of your face, and instead of looking there I rest my head on your chest, unaccustomed to your arms not returning my embrace.

Because stories keep us alive, I will tell you one as I rock back and forth on you. When my Tia Dolores was young in the Azores, she did not know how to tell her husband João that he made her heart swell beautifully, as if it owned the power of the sea. She painted him a medallion that would say this for her, with everything on it that she understood about water, its color and motion. She included fish with gaudy names, like the Moorish Idols and Blue Damsels and Sarcastic Fringeheads, and crowded in algae forests and every symbol that came to her. Layers and layers of shades were applied, until the medallion was solid black. But she did not see this, since she was determined to leave nothing out, and every scene that had gone into her work was clear to her.

João was delighted with her gift. That night he wore it around his neck at a garden party. She overheard him boasting to a guest that his wife had painted him this black medallion, and at first she was annoyed at him for not fully appreciating the complexities she had spent so much time pouring out of herself. But then she glimpsed her gift in the light of the pink lanterns strung on a clothesline, and she had to agree that the medallion shone not like some totality about aquatics, but like a dense stone. What wasted hours! The guests held up their glasses in the hot night, and the ice chasing itself in the glasses snapped as it died. Fireflies were like sea spray dotted over everyone's heads.

Ah! Ah! My wetness flows out to cover your thighs, with you buried inside me. You—oh, I thought you were reaching for me, but your muscles are merely twitching under my weight and— *Stop clawing parentheses in the air over your chest!* No one has ever survived to explain why the dying make those gestures.

Tia Dolores convinced herself that she had to paint a new medallion. Though she thought that she had learned what she needed to do and could finish something quickly, her many attempts turned out inadequate until she reached middle age, when she settled on painting a few fish in a kelp bed. She was exhausted and barely trusted herself to tell a good design from a bad one, although she had a vague sense of having taught herself to search out the solid, basic lines that would convey a sense of water.

João, kissing her all over, traded the blacked-out medallion he had worn faithfully for years for the new one. The simplicity of the painting was an improvement, in that it showed a willingness to wade through images until a single one that contained all the others could be found. On the other hand, no one looking at the new medallion had any way of feeling that it was supposed to be about love.

Tia Dolores was more determined than ever to get it right, but there followed a few decades of unsuccessful attempts. Not until she was old, sitting with João at Candlestick Park during a 49er football game, did she shout, "Finally!" It came to her, as the wind surged like an invisible tide, and a wide receiver dropped a desperation pass, that she had had to arrive here in the bleachers one winter, after years of knowing and feeling many things, in order to receive this inspiration. She did not comprehend exactly what needed to be done, only that she at last had come to the point of being able to do it. They went home fast, and—

My sweat bathes you. They claim that the tube forcing air in and out of you means your spirit has already fled, but I insist that something of you must remain. I must hurry.

—Dolores worked urgently. At any moment she might die, leaving the best medallion unfinished. The brushes leapt to meet her hands. She dissolved into a quietness, and the colors performed. João made tea and cooked dinner for many nights, but she refused to take in anything for fear it would block what was coming out of her.

She painted the finest love story made of water within her. She had heard it as a child, without sensing how to make it hers until now: Once on São Miguel, the largest island of the Azores, a princess was forbidden to marry her beloved shepherd. While telling him that she could never be his, she wept until a blue lake gushed out of her blue eyes. Grief seized him too, and his green eyes emptied out a green lake. She drowned herself in the lake he had made, and he threw himself into her lasting blueness. To this day, these lakes can be seen next to one another on São Miguel.

Dolores fit together a blue teardrop shape and an inverted green one. When that dried, she painted white waves over the blue and green background. She was convinced that if she were to distill whatever was magnificent in a human being, it would look like a white wave. She added two tiny figures of people as well, each carrying one of these waves. It did not matter whether any viewers of the medallion knew of the princess and the shepherd; it did not matter whether viewers would be able to say exactly what dancing waves did to their nerves. They would be able to feel, from the vibrancy of the shapes, that someone had lovingly—this was the story within the story—captured the ache of love.

When João saw this medallion, he wept, and so did anyone who came across it. They could all picture themselves, to varying degrees, and without perhaps being able to define the sensation in words, as having traveled to a wonderful place. They, too, stood on the edge of bodies of water created out of some agonizing passion. And the medallion shone always renewed and different, according to what it evoked out of others.

"Tell me," asked Tia Dolores, her voice trembling. "Tell me

why people are crying. Why am I?" She was not entirely certain what she had done.

"What a marriage of real and imagined things," said João, wiping the tears from his face, and from hers. "You have re-minded us that we have souls, Dolores."

I hear a doctor laughing outside. They want me to finish so that they can come in and disconnect you. I would like to shout the stories of everything you have done, James, and the sum total of everything you and I did together, with our dreams glossed over my recital, but no, that would be blacking out the medallion. Let this last moment in your room be the second medallion, direct and real. For the third, I must choose a story that will tell all our stories:

As a pastry chef you wore spotless clothing and dwelled where what is practical and what is inspired are forced to fit together into a shape. The first time I came into your shop, you served me a tart filled with cream. It looked like a pool on a day of glare. Very plain, but honest, as carefully selected food is said to be. You added only an oblong of pale, pale blue that flared on one end, a shape floating in the cream, a blue that everyone might not detect. It suggested, you told me, a whale. What was wonderful was how something as huge as a whale could be made very small and eaten practically whole.

"Why not make the blue darker, and the whale more obvious?" I asked. The stunning mass of your black hair distracted me.

"If I do that," you said, "people will see only what I thought, and it would be a sight and not a feeling. This way, customers can feel whatever they want."

But I decided that beautiful things must be declared much more boldly. When I worked with you, I placed gold foil stars under the tarts, and you let me do it.

Then I decorated them with sugar roses and insisted that you add orange flavoring to the cream, and you did it because you were going to help me learn on my own about creation.

To make the whales stand out, I traced their contours with red coloring, and used a toothpick to sketch in spouts. It was too much to think that customers would miss the point, or the care you took. The sales fell. I was puzzled.

You went back to a whisper of a blue spirit flowing in cream, lines that met at one end and then flared outward. How content you were day after day, engaged in the most fleeting of arts. Eaten; gone. Only now do I see that you were waiting for me to enter the realm of the Blue and Green Lakes. People must be drawn to a shoreline because they feel something there—something of a yearning, the unknown story. They stand there or jump in, radiant with their own barely visible feelings. Strange that it took me forever to realize that everyone fears death as much as I do.

Your truest stories are all imbedded in this story of the making of whales. Included would be your teaching me to leap in and not be afraid of swimming in the open water. To carry my yearning into the unpredictable ocean. That speaks of your patience, your ability to go into the world and to invite others to do the same, divining whatever they wish of it. You showed me in slow stages how to get past the waves until I no longer feared swimming out of my depth. I was secure with you—

This hideous room! I hate that soap smell that triggers fear in everyone. Patients should be able to leave their cards, the pressings of their carnations, and their journal entries taped to the walls, to comfort those who follow.

—Circling around me; you were not going to leave me. That was when you ignored your rule about never turning one's back on the force of water, and that wave roared up from behind to dash your head against the rocks.

Astonishing that after your brain has been declared dead, your ability to love goes on. I feel you come inside me.

I hardly remember them leading me away from you. You start to drip out of me, and I run into the ladies' room to lie on the cold tile with my legs up. Did you feel anything, I wonder, even though this was more about survival than desire? I must seize a child out of you; I had one last chance to create the child we dreamed of. This child will be you, you still walking on the earth. I fold my hands over my abdomen and command it to rise.

A week, ten days later, at the Castle Restaurant along the coast, I asked for an ocean seat. The waiter started to clear away the extra place setting, but he stopped. I was grateful. I wanted to ask him,

And you? What do you carry within, that has taught you how to read people with such tenderness?

"I'd like the stuffed mushrooms, the wild-greens salad, and the salmon. Wait, I'm very hungry. Can you add extra rice?" I said.

He made no joke about me feeding myself to some point of immobility. "Whatever you wish," he said. He was young, with a delicate face. Why do so many people think delicacy belongs to the fainthearted? How can it, requiring as it does so much chiseling?

"Wish? No," I said, "I can't stop to think about wishes. I'm eating for two."

He smiled discreetly, this savior sent to feed me. "Ask for whatever you want."

Looking out as the sunset was the blood-in-water pink that deepens to purple and then to the blacking-out that is the night, I felt the twinge every woman knows that signals pain is approaching, and nothing will stop a new cycle. My period would come quite soon, and with it not a child, but the end of you.

What did I want? Is that what the savior asked? Watching birds swooping out of the trees toward insects, I realized I was bad at naming what was in front of me. What were these birds, these insects? What should I call the trees?

"Tell me the name of those birds," I asked the waiter as he brought my mushrooms and greens.

"Birds? Those are bats," he said.

What we learn when we listen to others! I had read about bats, but having them as dinner companions was new to me. With my waiter in his white jacket behind me, we watched the bats swoop blind but graceful through the dark.

I discovered bats! This was one of the miracles assigned to me, though it was infinitely smaller, of course, than being granted a child. We have many chances for stories, only one chance to make a life. My finest miracle was James, and that he could love me after he was gone. I need to ask everyone: What are your miracles, and how are they different from the ones you planned for? Please tell me. You must tell everyone.

The cry of bats is too high-pitched for us to decipher, but I am here to tell you that if you happen to be screaming through the air with them, you will hear, as I did, that they are the messengers of the dead. They brought me James saying, "Do not turn from rocks, or death. I have laid down my life so that with every gesture you welcome something outside yourself."

I abandoned my dinner, went at once to the ocean, entered it, and glided like a bat in a dark water dance. Perhaps from the shore my outline was faint, a suggestion. It did not matter that I was as indistinct as one of his whales.

For a soul is not a thing. A soul is not even a thing secured unseen in a body. But this troubles me: Who can say how well a soul can live on, unless it is somehow found by a body, and put inside stories?

Those parentheses you clawed in the air with your fingers over your heart? Let me name the moment. You were telling me *enclose what is invisible, and then go on*. And I do, here now, so full of the water of you I am a prayer to bursting.

MY HUNT FOR KING SEBASTIÃO

Ah, quando quererás, voltando,
Fazer minha esperança amor?
Da nevoa e da saudade quando?
Quando, meu Sonho e meu Senhor?

[When will it be your will, returning
Here, to make, of my hope, love?
Ah, when, out of this mist and yearning?
When, Dream in me and Lord above?]

—Fernando Pessoa, "Third," from the cycle
"The Warnings," *Mensagem*. Jonathan Griffin,
translator

My girlfriend was a beautiful liar. I should say "is." I figure Cecilia is still inventing her answers off in the fog, or wherever it is that people go when we stop seeing them. She'd say things like, for instance, money wasn't important to her, but she sulked when I decided not to go to law school. Then she made it worse by saying that she wasn't bothered by anything except a headache. I asked her once to look at me, will you, and tell me one thing that's completely true. She had me craving plain facts, even tough ones. Not big truths, just facts to get me through the day.

Getting through his days was all my father wanted to do, and I could see why. My mother was another liar. One morning I dropped by the house, and she was smiling in a weird way. I gave her a few chances to tell me what was wrong, but she didn't let me in on anything. One week later, she left my father for another man. Whenever she and I spoke after that on the phone, it wasn't for long. I was stunned that this was the woman who raised me, and I didn't know the first thing about her. She wouldn't explain why she went, even when I practically begged her to.

My father didn't have much of a clue about my mother either. Anyway that was how it seemed at the time. My excuse was that I lived twenty miles away and came by for short visits only a few times a week. I had graduated from college three years before, and I admit that I was floating, waiting for what I was and what I should do to appear to me. Like Cecilia, my father was disappointed (probably my mother was too) that I seemed content with paralegal work. It was a job. A lot of paperwork, a hunt after details, but I didn't have to get up in front of a judge and defend someone I knew was guilty, which my father has often had to do.

My father was a quiet man, well-groomed, and he stayed like that after my mother ran off, except that he entered a deeper kind of silence, where someone goes after a revelation. He seemed grayer at the edges, but that could have been age. I started coming over several nights a week to make dinner for him and turned into the docile child he never had, grilling meat and fixing salads that he never ate. At first I let him eat and drink some wine and not say much. If you're taught that action is accomplishment and accomplishment is emotion, then lack of action or speech gets to be how men take sorrow out of events. It's not lying; it's mourning peacefully. My father screaming and crying—that wasn't who he was.

Instead, he told me, one night at the dinner table, a funny story about another lawyer in his Portuguese society, the I.D.E.S., or *Irmandade do Divino Espírito Santo*, the Brotherhood of the Holy Ghost. This lawyer kept records about the money he was embezzling from his firm, and I'll leave it to you to suggest why this jerk stored these papers in a safe in his house. When his partners uncovered his tracks, he set fire to his home, his entire home—I'm not kidding—to destroy the trail. As if the walls were breathing what the truth was, and he had to get rid of the walls, and the Holy Ghost was mad and sending down tongues of fire. The one thing that survived the flames was his fire-proof safe. It stood in the scorched field, with the evidence inside needed to send him to prison. That's true guilt at work. Also proof that nothing can stay hidden forever.

We laughed. Dad told the story again, and we laughed again, although a little less. Rachmaninoff played in the background. Some people say that he has an easy, loud grandness, for unrefined tastes. But my father loved the largeness of the chords, and so did I, especially after I read that Rachmaninoff dreamt one night that he was trapped inside his coffin, and he was going wild trying to get out, and his music drew its strength from that. It could've been the arsonist proclaiming, "Discover me!" and Rachmaninoff's "Release me!" that made me blurt, "Dad, you should do things. You know," and I paused, not wanting to say "get on with your life." If a person is alive, that's exactly what he's doing. We put a time limit on grief and want the person to be frantic for our sakes. Action being accomplishment being emotion.

He put down his knife and fork, and dabbed his lips with the linen napkin I'd set out. No folded paper towels for us, no sir, we were draining the cup of merriment. "What should I do, do you think, Dean?"

"I don't know, Dad." I didn't.

"I haven't missed a day of work."

"Then tell me about one of your cases," I said. My father has worn a tie to the dinner table since I can remember, and this grace brought unfailingly to what requires none was finally beginning to break my heart.

He sighed. "Let's see." His mind wandered off, trying to edit his days into something that I might find interesting.

"Never mind, Dad," I said.

"The Portuguese sailed around the world and opened the route to the East, Dean," he said, cutting his steak into neat squares, "and now, as the poet Fernando Pessoa and many others have said, we've done nothing for the last four hundred years but talk about it."

"Meaning what, exactly?"

"Meaning that history swings back and forth, and not everyone has to be dashing around every living minute."

"Then we must be in the part where we talk about it," I said. Silence.

"She's not coming back, Dad," I said. "Not ever."

"I assume you mean your mother."

I noticed the dish towel over my shoulder, from fixing dinner. I flung it backward onto the counter. "Cecilia isn't either, if that's what you mean," I said. "Have some salad."

"I hate salad."

"I'm trying to make you see—"

"How do you *know* she's not coming back? You don't know everything," said my lawyer father, looking straight through me.

"I don't know how I know, I just do." I couldn't say that it had to do with her face, with flesh twisted in a direction I didn't recognize. I wanted plain facts, but there's such a thing as kindness. My take on matters then was that my father was gentle and tidy, more than my mother ever was, and I had gone and wrecked his peace. He had this composed nervousness that made me want to protect him, and I'd betrayed that, too. His arguments in the courtroom the few I'd heard—were eloquent, as if he could shout honor into the sky, which is so hopeless and noble that from my childhood on I've been afraid of him dying, terrified of him having to face death some day, because he would have to watch it knock down what he believed about hope and honor; as we're all aware, death cares about neither. I feared death for him more than I did for anyone else I knew or have known since.

But I didn't know my father that well, not really, outside of the basic outline. He'd come to this country when he was eighteen from the island of Terceira in the Azores; in my whole life the one memory he'd shared with me was that the breezes that came in off the sea made him decide at a very young age to dedicate himself to matters of the air, to the intellect and rightness, and to him that translated into a study of the law. That's how I saw my father as an immigrant—light and indistinct, but burning, burning. He married my mother, a native Californian of Italian and German descent, after meeting her at the All Saints Church fair in Hayward, and they were determined to be unethnic, in the style of their time. They named me Dean, because they wanted me to make the dean's list some day. Other than the Holy Ghost festival every year, and my hazy certainty that any girl refusing the honor of being named Queen would be struck dead within the year, my only link to what I was on my father's side, other than seeing in my mind that princely and ghostly immigrant that he had been, was to speak my broken Portuguese with him now and then. I was mostly self-taught. And I was, at least tangentially, part of the Lusitanian community, a Luso-American—Portugal being called *Lusitania* by the ancient Romans.

Nowadays people like to claim that they're the product—and I mean exactly that—of the land of their ancestors; it suggests ceremonies and royalty and flights of fancy, more glamorous than the shopping lists we make of our days. I'm like that myself. My parents wanted to be American, but people my age want to take the most exotic portion of their blood and paint themselves a character out of it. The problem is that we collect quick impressions and pretend that they're sensations we've earned. I plead guilty to that as much as the next guy should. But I do have one Lusitanian quality that has the strength of instinct in me, without my faking it or pumping it up: Portuguese fatalism gravitates to the absolute. The lawyer setting fire to his house could see no future except what had materialized before him. In this brand of fatalism, there is a grand event allotted to each person—only one, with every other major event a consequence of that—and from this grand event will spring that person's lasting description. A Luso-American cousin of mine in the agricultural heat of Manteca had a married lover who'd given her a son, and she was grim and dignified about needing to live to the end in this blurred state of incompleteness. To us Americans, the resting place that will be our happiness is always farther on (but not too far), past the visible horizon. We're always waiting for ourselves to show up, in other words, and at the same time never allowing that to happen. We're eager to disown whatever generic sense that being American might mean, while not wanting to surrender its privileges.

I assumed that my mother's leaving was my father's grand event. I hadn't discovered yet that it wasn't, that there was another one out there. (As for mine, I figured it wouldn't catch up to me for a while. I can say now, maybe warn you, though probably you've already figured as much, that if you find yourself thinking that you've got years to go before meeting yours, it's getting ready to come along and sink its teeth into you.) It turned out that my father had other things on his mind, besides my mother and fatalism and getting on with his life. He asked if I were familiar with the bit of land in the Azores that he'd inherited from his father.

Are you at home, pleased to find yourself reading, because who knows where the hours escape? See the doorway? My Vô's plot was about the size of what's in front of you, but my father was receiving about three letters a month, from the Borges branch of his family, or the Almeidas, or the Ferreiras, demanding that he give it to one of them. He'd given it years before to his Tia Mafalda, and since she had died recently the letters were arriving with different degrees of heat and cross-accusations. Long ago my father had instructed Mafalda to decide on her own who should get the land after her, and to leave him out of it, but no one was writing him with the straight story of what she'd done or not done. He explained all this, and stopped, watching me.

"Yes?" I said. Having broken the tranquillity of our evenings by prescribing getting on with his life, I was going to have to pay.

"They're driving me crazy," he said.

I said I'd go get the truth for him. Going away would be for the best. I was tired of cooking and pretending that I didn't miss Cecilia.

He promised he'd buy my ticket and give me some pocket money, plus fifty dollars for the priest at the Mãe de Deus Church in Angra do Heroísmo, his old parish, to have a Mass offered for our dead.

"No problem," I said. "Thanks." A minor errand for a relatively free holiday.

"You don't have to do this," he said.

"I have plenty of vacation days saved up."

He mentioned that he would write to Tio David, who worked for TAP, or Transporto Aéreo Portugal, the airline. Tio David appeared neutral in the battle for the land, and I could stay with him.

My father and I finished our dinner. When his face met mine, he looked happy—not so much because our gazes were momentarily passing over each other, a rarity, but because, it struck me, my company had become a burden. I didn't blame him. It's hard to dream aimlessly when someone is demanding that you become constructive. He would continue wearing his tie when he was dining by himself; he wasn't going to collapse without me. He wanted peace. From me and my mother and his relatives and the demanding earth.

"I'll do it," I repeated. We have to choose whatever words we can when the moment of declaring "I love you" vanishes before we can own up to it.

Vanished such words remain, although I think more and more that the body of what we do and fail to do lingers in the atmosphere. I was reminded of this as my plane was descending—what a feeling, to be a flying creature entering the fog, scanning it for shapes and traces of some message. Fog is the same shroud worn in the mornings by California—*my homeland, my arid California, how predictably badly you are aging. We wait for something, someone, to rise up and save you from what you are.*

I leaned back, alarmed at this sad song that had burst into my head. Where did it come from? As the wings cut lower through the clouds, I imagined that the underside of each of the nine islands would look moist and stringy, like a giant mushroom's. I was nostalgic for this place where I'd never been.

On the ground, inside the small terminal, were dozens of men in suits and ties, anticipating our plane in Lajes, not far from the American air base. Our landing was an event, rather than an errand. Passengers applauded the pilot before crowding toward the doors. I waited for my two cloth bags, and stood near a door left open to equalize the humidity indoors and out. My fellow travelers had huge suitcases and steamer trunks with twine and belts around them in case the locks (magically) broke. I had a surge of fondness for people who did not trust even the simplest closing mechanisms. Men lit cigarettes and focused on some faraway point. Suddenly I noticed that I was no longer in the best position to grab my luggage, but behind everyone else. Aha, I thought, seeing the pack of middle-aged women in front of me; my first instance of falling victim to the bosom wedge. My god-father had once explained that a certain stout brand of women, not perceptive enough to grasp that they are mad at the world, will tilt their massive chests into an opening in a crowd, and where a sizable shelf goes the rest of the body will follow. Young men back off deferentially, and then it dawns on them they've been breasted aside. I didn't care. It gave me a couple of extra minutes to wonder how I would find an uncle I'd never met, this uncle who was going to be a host, guide, the patron saint I never got because my parents named me Dean.

A man in a dark suit, his back to me, had a sweat wrinkle like an arrow creasing his jacket. I relied on that. I'm not sure why, maybe because it was like an X on a map. "Tio David," I said.

He turned, threw down his cigarette, kissed one side of my face and then the other, grabbed my bags, and led me out to an old Buick, which he said he'd bought from a retiring major at the base. David was talking fast, but I could pick out the crests in his sentences.

I tasted the clean air greedily, the way Californians do: here sweet, there smoky. The streets were knobby with black and white cobblestones, and the houses were low and whitewashed, with religious tiles set like jewels over the doors. David's driving wasn't giving me a chance to soak up more than that. He was speeding around the blind curves. The seat belts didn't work. He was cheerful. Being short and slight, he probably figured he could sidle around solid objects without worrying.

"Nice houses," I said.

"These?" He looked momentarily annoyed. "Huh! Everybody piled up together!" He was facing me as he spoke.

I gestured forward to indicate that it was not necessary for him to turn his full attention on me while he drove.

"Don't worry," he said. "No one will bother you at my house."

"I'm not expecting any trouble," I said.

He said nothing, and took another curve close to the wall. I could have sworn the oncoming car passed through the Buick.

His home on the outskirts of the capital city of Angra do

Heroísmo was out of my boyhood fantasies—large and with weathered stones and vines, including rust-colored ones, shielding the façade. A muddy creek, which I instantly enlarged into a moat, snaked through the overgrown front yard. From the flat rooftop, I would be able to stare out at the ocean.

"*Chega!*" declared Tio David, which is not merely "he or she or it arrives," but what you'd say when a waiter has brought plenty, or when an incident reaches surfeit. He tossed my bags down in a dark foyer that had a red velvet wall hanging, a further inlay of richness in the darkness. It looked like the home of every Azorean relative I had in California, with tiny windows and no lights switched casually on.

"My wife Marilda and my son Leonel," Tio David said, and a short, round woman appeared, holding the hand of a six- or seven-year-old boy. Marilda was older than David. Her hair was parted in the middle and curved toward her chin. After David kissed her and their son, and I followed his lead, there was a gracious flurry of questions about my trip, my health, and my father, and afterward I was shown to my room.

My plan was to nap, then spend an uneventful evening with my uncle and his family. I could practice not translating everything into English in my head first before translating my replies into Portuguese. The following day I would interview the first half of the list of ten names that my father had given me. Angra was new to me, but I figured I could get around easily. The second half of my list could be covered the day after, and on the third day—or the fourth, allowing for the unforeseeable—I would make my judgment about the rightful owner of the land. The rest of my vacation I could spend drinking beer and pursuing a romance: but I fell into an extraordinary sleep. I awoke to find a basket of sweetbread and apples and a knife on my bedside table. I ate everything, but when I tried to part the curtains to let in daylight, they were so fragile that I tore them just from touching them, not big tears, but enough to send me back to bed. Much too soon I was doing things for which I had to compose apologies.

Eating the apple peels was a mistake. The one bathroom was attached to the kitchen and could only be reached by passing through there. David and Marilda were at the breakfast table as witnesses whenever I ran into the bathroom. We were forced into friendly smiles and nods. It was ghastly. I imagined briefly that I had come here to die. The courtyard was right outside the bathroom wall, and I got to listen to my uncle and aunt freely discussing my distress and its probable causes with visitors. I hoped none of them happened to be a petitioner for the land. Whenever I washed my hands and saw my reflection, I was impressed and scared at how fast I could get this wan.

After this spell was concluded, I returned the empty basket, thereby committing my first *ofensa*, unless you want to count shredding the curtains. I had not returned full what had been given to me full. If Marilda cared, she didn't show it. She pushed up her large hexagonal glasses and ushered me into the dining room. They had been patiently waiting for me to be able to stomach a huge meal. Silver, china, and crystal glasses of wine sat on a lace tablecloth. We made small talk over the kale-and-potato soup, with Leonel staring at me and giggling when I spoke incorrectly. The subject of the land was avoided. It was, however, the enormous unstated presence, like another person sitting at the table. Clearly they were going to be hospitable but didn't want to get involved, though they might enjoy my gossip about it later on. David and Marilda had crammed their chairs together at one head of the table, not just to give me the other head but so that they could eat leaning toward each other. I couldn't name why I found them splendid and agonizing to look at, until it came to me that I was an adult finally realizing that I had never seen my parents touch each other.

We finished a whole baked fish covered with orange juice and nuts, followed by a roast. Salad was sliced tomatoes and onions with oil and unpitted olives. I ate boundlessly, immensely, as if I would waft away unless I weighted myself down. Dessert was a staggering pile of meringue and whipped cream over strawberries, which David said was called "Himalaya." The *h* was silent, and I was a little drunk by then, and David had to repeat the name four times before I understood. As I sipped some port, I stared bleary-eyed and full of goodwill at the large bookcases crowded with volumes. Books lined most of the walls in the house.

"Guess you don't like to read very much," I said.

David looked at his wife, then at me. "No, I love reading," he said mildly, gesturing at the books. Marilda was squinting at me, as we do when we aren't sure we've heard something right. The eyes attempt to read on the air what the ears failed to report accurately.

"That's what I meant," I said, feebly.

Leonel giggled.

"Well!" I said. "What a banquet!" I repeated this several times, which seemed to smooth things over. "Tomorrow I'll start with the Almeidas. First on my list."

David shook his head. "There's a festival tomorrow. Our Lady of the Stars of Heaven. It'll be hard to find them, unless you catch them at the running of the bulls. And sorry, you're on your own there."

I perked up. "Bulls?"

David shrugged. "In the Praça de República. Not for me."

"I'd like to go," I said.

"Go, then," said David.

"I won't know how to find my relatives unless they're at home. Won't you—"

A strong gust of wind silenced me by blowing through and slamming a door shut.

"It's Sebastião!" said David, and he and Marilda clasped hands and laughed. "Sebastião will help you!"

When I asked who Sebastião was, Leonel, bored, asked to be excused.

David explained that Sebastião was the young king whose body was never found on the battlefield of Alcácer-Quibir, and he was supposed to ride in one day on the mist, a messiah who would restore the lost glory of Portugal. Whenever a fog rolled in, adherents of Sebastianismo went to the shoreline to await him. David added, unnecessarily, that for many people this was not a religion so much as a welcome excuse to sit and visit.

While clearing away the dishes, Marilda remarked quite pleasantly that David was going to a party to meet his girlfriend, and now that I was well, I could go out and socialize too. It was my turn to squint. David had risen from the table and was plucking his hat off the ornate hat rack. To clear up any misunderstanding, she added that only yesterday she'd had a special mattress delivered to the girlfriend's house. David had a bad back, poor dear. He came over and kissed Marilda warmly, and when he looked at me every word of my Portuguese fell out of my brain. I relied on gestures to suggest that I was incapacitated from the meal. The thought of my own parents living as blithely under such intrigue was dizzying. After David went out, I helped Marilda with the dishes. She had lots of questions about life in California. She was remarkable, although she wouldn't have thought so. I tried picturing my own mother like this, this calm, and couldn't. My mother was the kind of woman who had affairs because she feared her husband beating her to it. Leaving my father for another man had to do with bitterness and competition. No wonder Tio David didn't care a damn about bullfights or my Vô's land. He had his stone castle, his wife, his secret life now on a better mattress; he ate Himalayas and didn't get fat.

I awoke remembering that I had money to deliver for the dead of our family. All at once, since I had lost a day in traveling, it was the start of my fourth day here, and time was slipping away. David and Marilda, their heads together, were in the dining room, laughing over their morning coffee. How bizarre a normal scene looks, when pasted over the hidden truth—to me, I mean. They looked unruffled. Her face was smooth as a breeze. I didn't meet David's eyes as I took some coffee from Marilda, who greeted me buoyantly. What unnerves us is being required to consider unseen things, such as the profound connection of spirits such as theirs.

"Morning," I muttered.

"This morning I'm going to give you a tour of the island," said David, slapping the table to demonstrate his enthusiasm.

Exasperation had me ready to split out of my skin. "I really need to find the Almeidas." At this rate there would be no leisurely seductions in a café. David wasn't going to be the only Romeo.

"I told you, it's the feast of Our Lady of the Stars of Heaven." He sounded insulted.

I submitted to another driving session with David, with him assuring me that I'd have time to deliver my father's money to Father Prado. The island went by fast, in jungle-like patches, but honestly it began to swim together, my fault, because I have never been good at enjoying what I think is keeping me from a direct purpose. When we arrived in the village of Biscoitos, so named because the lava spills look like raw biscuit dough, David insisted that there was an abyss I had to see. He was right. It was at last a moment in which I forgot myself. It was the holiest place I had ever been, with its churning white water and jellyfish bobbing up and down, slowly, opening and closing, like souls coming out of the depths. No one could hope to survive either the water or the stinging of the jellyfish, and that made everything more magnificent. David stood next to me, looking dashing with the jacket of his suit hanging off his shoulders, the empty arms lifting in the sea air. It must have been written on me, how much I needed this. I wanted to wire my father and inform him that he must come visit. In short, I killed the moment by musing what action, well-intended though it was, I should bring to it.

David needed to get to work, and he dropped me off near Father Prado's church, Mãe de Deus. I went half-mad trying to find him, with people giving conflicting directions because they didn't want to be rude and say they didn't know where he was, the theory being that any step forward, even a misguided one, kept the pursuit vital. It took me a while to figure this out. I found him, a kind but sickly man with a pillow over his stomach, lying on a bench in the Jardim Municipal, at the opposite end of Angra from his church. Red azaleas bloomed near his head, like fiery thoughts. He didn't move from his prone position as I pressed the envelope with my father's alms into his hand.

"I'm Dean Borges," I said. "This is for my father, Jaime Borges. Could you say a Requiem for our family, Father?"

"Today's the festival. I'll do it tomorrow. Three o'clock," he said, not bothering to open his eyes.

I paused, wondering if I'd been dismissed. "OK," I said. "Say, Father. You getting a tan?"

"No, I am resting."

I made a mental note to forget about sarcasm. My mood was lightening. I had taken care of one errand, and word of my presence was sure to get around to my relatives. In the meanwhile, I was going to watch a running of the bulls. I could adapt. After ordering a coffee in a restaurant, I drank from a white cup and studied the ocean, a framed rectangle at the end of the cobbled road lined with homes. I pictured the jellyfish ascending and descending. I bought a filigree charm at a jeweler's, with loosely formed hopes about a future girlfriend, and saw David pass by in the street with other men in blue TAP airline jackets. We waved. How had he managed to afford his house? Festival day or not, he didn't act as if he worked very hard.

At noon, crowds began gathering in the praça. Families with picnic baskets climbed onto the walls separating the square from a narrow street lined with homes. Some boys used the flower planters in the middle of the square to hoist themselves into trees. Milling around were the obvious emigrants in their American clothes, back here for a visit. Many of them bought some of the 22-carat gold. The Azores was a place, like Ireland, where people grew up to leave, and out in the villages today flags were being raised to show where the children of the house had gone. Mostly they went to Canada now, and there would also be Brazilian, American, and French flags, like faraway dreams waving in the breeze.

A bank of long concrete steps was built against the backside of a solid stretch of homes opposite from the families with their picnics. I had no problem being a coward, and settled onto a top step, about ten up from the street. No one sat in the first four rows. The expectancy in the air made me forget, slightly, about the land.

When a horn sounded, you'd have thought that heaven had dropped acid into the middle of the square. Everyone on the ground jumped toward the perimeter. Some of the waiting men held umbrellas open and ready. A woman two rows in front of me handed me a bottle of wine. My heart was pounding. There was a long wait without animals. The sun was hot and direct. Leaves fell; the boys in the trees were kicking the branches. Women in the balconies above our steps were leaning on the quilts they'd hung from the wrought-iron railings. My skin started to crawl, not only on account of my getting to see something I'd never seen before, but because I noticed that the praça and the exit were now indefinitely closed to me. I'd never liked being hemmed in, but it was too late to change my mind.

The first bull trotted into the square, and the crowd pointed and the excitement rolled up and broke over us. A man flashed a blanket, and the bull lowered its head and charged. Barely dodging a horn wrapped in a spongy bandage, the man allowed the bull to dart past and bowed to the applause. The bull continued through the praça, heading for the ring. I tapped the woman's shoulder to indicate that I wanted more wine. She passed it back to me, and I thanked her.

When another bull entered from the west and another from the north, I sat up straighter, surprised. They were being released on all sides. I don't know what I'd imagined, more of a column of bulls charging through in a raucous but orderly line—manageable trouble—as with cattle in a roundup. Then out of nowhere everything was happening too fast for me to contain it. One bull caught a man from behind while he was recoiling from one charging directly at him. He was tossed into the air, but after he fell the bull went after someone else. A bull released from the top of the residential street across the way destroyed, in two head-butts, a plywood guard built around a garden, and the bull tore through the garden and knocked its head against a front door. Another bull rammed into a tree in the center of the square, and the boys above clutched the limbs and screamed. One boy almost lost his footing, and the women in the balcony yelled for someone to distract the bulls and get them away from the children. I sat there, my spine rigid, knowing that if one of them fell, I would depend on someone else to come to his rescue, and that I was going to have to live with that, from now on. A man waving his arms hit the rear of the bull shaking the tree of boys, and the bull turned on him. He tried to run, but it slammed him against a flower planter, trapping him there. I flung up my arms stupidly and shouted. The bull smashed him again, and a spray of blood jetted up in the space between the bull's nostrils and the flowers. I grabbed the wine bottle from the woman and threw it into the street, which did nothing but make her mad and add another hazard for the men running around looking for a way out or up, up to safety. Five men teamed up to slap the bull from behind— and now there were more bulls running around—and the slapped bull went after the men and they scattered, while the man pinned to the flower planter staggered up. He no longer had a face. Part of a cheekbone shone white through the blood. Another bull was racing straight for the bank of steps where I was. Out of sheer fright the people on the steps below were carried backward and up and I was pressed high against the stucco wall. I tried to locate the woman who'd given me the wine—strange how slight the gestures are that forge an alliance—but I'd lost her. A broadside of muscle rammed into the steps in front of where I was trapped in this crush of yelling people, and after the bull went on, I saw a man lying face down in the street, his feet pointing inward, pigeon-toed.

"That man is hurt!" a woman called from the balcony.

Again I had a chance to go to the ground and battle it out and save someone, and again I waited for someone else to do it. I stared at the spectacle and wished myself away and thought, Fuck Hemingway. Fuck all easy moments of truth. Then: Jesus. Jesus. Then: *Sebastião, Sebastião: Will you refuse to save me, now that I've discovered I'm afraid to die for another man, for a child? For strangers?* But I would risk death to get away myself, and I ran along the top grade of steps, to the end. A truck was parked across the entrance to a street a few meters away, to keep the bulls from entering the city. I threw myself down, into danger for a heartbeat as I ran to the truck and squeezed around it, and my leg felt the hot muscle of one of the bulls passing by me. I sank down on the other, the safe, side of the truck.

I forget how many beers I had at the waterfront bar. As the evening wore on, no one could tell me whether that man on the ground was alive or dead. The ones who hated bullfighting shrugged, and the ones who loved it posed, with justifiable impatience, some questions for me. What exactly had I expected? Especially since I had seated myself that close to the ground. Had I just arrived on the planet and discovered that people everywhere held to rituals, to race-car driving or football or bullfighting, that might pose risk or danger?

There was no arguing with that. Here I was, the tourist in search of color without its historical price tag—that is, being owned, *transfigured* by that very history. Infiltrators want to collect pieces of it, like souvenirs off a beach, nothing more. We often do something for the sole purpose of reporting back at large what we've done and seen. Bullfights rank in the top of enviable actions to flash around out of our dossiers.

I concentrated on my beer and telling myself that it was too late to repeat my first test concerning whether I would save a stranger. Already I knew I wouldn't do anything differently if I had to do it over. As a teenager at the beach in California, I'd been alert toward the children in the surf, children I didn't know. I had been ready to go to the bottom after them if I needed to. I thought that's what I was made of, and now I wasn't sure. This didn't feel like the one grand event of my life, not yet, but today was going to be a tissue overlay on whatever was before me, that much I had gathered.

It must have been Sebastião who carried me back to David's house. Otherwise I can't explain how I woke up the next day with Marilda knocking on my door, holding out a cup of coffee. Leonel was peering at me from under her arm.

"Sorry," I said. The entire room was off its moorings, tilting.

I must have sounded fierce. Marilda and Leonel glanced sideways at one another. The inside of my skull was wet paper.

"Do you want anything?" she said, setting the coffee down on my night stand. "It's Wednesday, and today's the open-air market."

"Wednesday!" I said, sitting up too quickly. "Is Tio David here? Wednesday! I need a ride!" Today I would accomplish what I had come here to do, and let the gavel fall. I fumbled in the night stand for my list of names and addresses.

"He's at work," she said gently. "It's almost three o'clock."

"In the afternoon?" I screeched. "God!" My stay was almost

half over. Then a worse thought crowded in: the Mass! The Mass for the dead!

Marilda drove me to Mãe de Deus, with Leonel turning around occasionally in the front seat, eager for the next strange thing I would do. I leapt out in front of the church and wished them good luck at the market. I ran inside. Father Prado was already at the offertory. Obviously this was to be a service without any flourishes. The two back pews were filled, but otherwise the church was empty; the emptiness was ringing, without enough bodies to absorb the words coming from the priest. I threw myself into a midway pew and onto the kneeler, an uncushioned wooden plank. I'm not particularly religious, but Azorean crucifixes, with the skin peeled back around Christ's knees, and the splatters from the crown of thorns downward, do demand that we think of torture and hurt and our last end, and of: *Can you not watch with me for one hour, without falling asleep?* At the same time, it is not an age of faith. We shift our yearning for transcendence into a wish for accomplishments and traveling to other lands. My grand philosophizing was interrupted by the sense that the people in the last pews were staring holes into the back of my head. Of course. My relatives.

After Father Prado's final blessing came across as a banishing wave of his hand, he tried to exit through the back, but the worshippers blocked him and pointed at me, and I was thrown into an unexpected arena. They were shouting. Here in its loud glory was the moment I'd come for, but I was glancing around for a way out. This wasn't how it was meant to go, and I was caught between the wall built of their sound sweeping over and behind me, and another wall they had made of their bodies. At first I couldn't distinguish who they were, much less what they were yelling, though I picked out a few curses, including, "May you die with your eyes rolled upward!" I think this was directed at one of my cousins and not at me. My hand gripped the warm wood of the pew. If I didn't go closer, they were going to come over and shake an answer out of me. Father Prado, a stick attempting to beat back a gale, was laying his hand on the arms of people whose stories I was hurriedly working to match with their appearances:

The older man with my father's fair skin and strong jaw was probably Carlos Borges, his uncle, whose son had gone to Brazil to discover gold and had instead jumped off a cliff. (The son had given Carlos his life's grand event.) The two middle-aged women in long black dresses who resembled one another were probably Mafalda's two sisters, Ermelinha and Maria José. The youngest woman I figured would be Claudia, a cousin on my father's mother's in-law's side and a widow since her husband had died without warning at age twenty-five. The others, around ten or twelve of them, were a puzzle.

"Stop! All of you! I'm right here," I said, hurrying to the back of the church.

"Your Portuguese is terrible," said Carlos, obviously ruling out flattery as a means of persuasion. "Your father didn't raise you right."

"Leave my father out of this," I said.

"See?" said Carlos. "Terrible."

"Outside! Outside!" pleaded Father Prado, but they ignored him.

"I'm sorry your father is in a wheelchair," said a man I couldn't place, "but when I talked to him last week, he said that he and Mafalda wanted me to have the land."

"My father is *not* in a wheelchair!" I threw someone's hand off my wrist.

"Yes, he is," said the man.

"My God! Don't you think I should know about my own father?" I was yelling myself.

"Outside!" said Father Prado.

"He called *me* up," said a woman. "Poor man. He sounded ill. I'm good with plants, Senhor Borges." She burst into tears. "All I want is to grow some string beans! Is that so much?"

Father Prado gave her a handkerchief and told her to go home.

"Well?" Carlos said to me. "Now you can't speak at all?"

"It should go to *me*," said one of Mafalda's sisters.

"Why her and not me?" said the other sister, pulling me close enough to peer into her eyes.

"Let go," I said.

"I'm sorry your father is on his deathbed, but that means you have to be the one to decide," said a man. "Since your brother can't!"

"My father is not on his deathbed, and I don't have a brother!" I shouted. My father could have solved everything by giving me, his rightful heir, the land—but it was as if he already had known that I would discover that I could be as romantic as I liked, and I'd never belong here, at least not with any take-it-or-leave-it ease. It was poetic justice that I was in a scene like this, with feuding cousins, arguments over land, and waving arms: Crude forms are what a visitor and not a native first sees. A bullfight, a brightly-hued quarrel. What materializes is often exactly what one deserves, at the level he deserves it.

"You're rich," said either Ermelinha or Maria José. "Buy the land and give it to one of us."

"I am not rich," I said.

"Sure you are," said someone.

"No, I'm not."

"You are," said the woman who seemed to be Carlos's wife. "How else could you afford to fly here?"

"That's right," said a sister.

"I don't need you to agree with me!" snapped Carlos's wife.

I looked at Claudia for help. She was on the edge of this flurry, studying me but saying nothing.

"Everyone calm down," said Father Prado. He turned to me and said, "Decide. Anything."

"All right," I said, the American son of the American lawyer. "We'll settle this right now. Who has the original deed? If Tia Mafalda signed over anything, that should be it."

They reached into various pockets and withdrew documents, some with ribbons, very embellished and impressive. I received them in my outstretched hand.

"Good-bye," said Father Prado, disgusted with me. How much could it cost to obtain a fancy, stamped paper? Any local official could have been persuaded to issue one for a price. Eliminating the false deeds would be impossible. One was as valid and invalid as the next. I performed the one act I could think of, as they stared anxiously. I fled. My blood is thick and American; I gripped the evidence, and I outdistanced them.

At a restaurant down an alley, I cowered in the back and ordered a steak with a fried egg and potatoes and a half-bottle of wine. On the walls were *azulejos,* the blue and white tiles that look like formations and reformations of clouds and heaven. A blue ship was sailing on a cream sea. I smoothed the deeds out on the table, but the restaurant was dark, and I could read what was on them only dimly. Not that that mattered. If there were any truths to discover, I already had: when the bulls came racing in, and I ran off; when the relatives I wanted to belong to came at me, and I ran away, to digest; when I needed a vacation from my father's grief.

Or that was what I was set to conclude. When I looked up and saw Claudia, I sat back, incredulous, trapped again. I'd had plenty. *Chega.* How had she divined where to find me? One frank grace of island life, like it or not, had to be this ultimate impossibility of a clean get-away.

She sat across from me, hesitating.

"If it's about the land, you can take it. I don't care," I said. She hadn't said anything in the church, and I supposed now she was here to make her case. The rest of them would come rushing in at any second.

"No, no. I wanted to give you this," she said, opening her purse and handing me a photograph. It was of a young man who looked like me—younger, but at the same time more ancient on account of the beige and oyster-like tinge of the photo. He wore a suit with a high collar and directed his attention off to the side, but he had my forehead, as wide and smooth as a sheet of paper, my large eyes, my poorly combed hair. Another cousin; I was about to receive his deed as well.

"OK," I sighed, handing the photograph back. "Let's have it."

"When I saw your face in the church, I knew you were looking for him."

"Whatever you say." I waited.

She pressed the photograph into my hand again and said, "Keep it. You need to. I know you don't have any pictures of your brother."

"I don't have any pictures of my brother because I don't have a brother," I said, repeating what I had said to the man in the church.

She touched the stem of my wineglass; she guided a bead of moisture up the side of the glass until it disappeared beneath her finger.

"How could I be looking for someone who doesn't exist?" I insisted, but my mind was working fast. My father hadn't left here until he was eighteen. It was possible, mathematically possible, that he'd had a child he wasn't aware of; certainly he hadn't mentioned any brothers to me. It didn't seem like a scenario from the life of the father I knew, but it was not out of the question. Unless this was part of some elaborate argument as to why Claudia deserved the land, I couldn't understand why she'd go to this much trouble to shock me. I said, "I'll tell my father."

She shook her head. She recited a story, then, that I hadn't expected. She could tell that it clearly was news to me. I heard what she was saying, but I couldn't reply, I couldn't even formulate any questions. For my father to have told me nothing, to have never mentioned that he had another history, seemed a cruel omission that he, in his mildness, did not appear capable of; but then I was not always generous and capable myself, whether at bullfights or disputes or elsewhere. Claudia told me that my father had been married at seventeen here in the islands, and that his wife died after giving birth to a son—the boy in the photo. No one blamed my father for being incapable of caring for his boy properly after that, but he promised to do what was right. He would leave this place, with its air roaring with spirits, and when he could afford it, he would send for his son. In the meantime, Tia Mafalda would raise the child. Once again no one blamed my father as the years passed, since they agreed that his heart had abandoned him. When he finally sent word that he had his law degree and his son could come live with him, the boy was accustomed to living with Tia Mafalda and refused to go. He was an engaging child, and then an optimistic and farsighted teenager, and everyone wept a great deal when he died at sixteen of influenza.

"Don't be angry with your father," said Claudia. "His pain killed him very young."

I tried to grin at her. He had sent me here to stumble across this, rather than tell me himself. Like the lawyer who found it easier to burn down his house than state the history of what he had done. "How did you get so good at figuring out what people are thinking? I guess you really can read faces."

Her scrutiny was unrelenting.

"But I don't know why you're telling me this," I said.

She reached out and put her hands near both my ears, until I was looking directly at her. "Because you look haunted. Anyone can see that. Because you inherited the haunted look of your father. I thought if you knew why, it would help."

"I see," I said, but I didn't. That I could look at my father day after day, for years, and not see him! I collected the false deeds and the photo of my dead half-brother and put them in my pocket. I had to get out of there. I signaled for the waiter to take my plate and bring my bill. As I put money on the table, Claudia hadn't moved.

"Thank you for your trouble," I said. "I'd like to go home now. Back to David's, I mean. I don't know what to tell you about the land. Sorry."

She wouldn't quit staring at me.

"Unless you have another bomb you'd like to drop," I said, getting to my feet.

She stood and leaned toward me, kissing me with lips like dried leaves; it was the most sorrowful kiss I'd ever received. "Will you do me the kindness," she whispered, "of reading my face?"

"What?"

"Please."

Her forehead was against mine. I took her face in both my hands. Other people in the restaurant were beginning to notice us, and I wasn't sure what to say. "Your husband—your husband was so young when he died, and—"

"That's something everyone already knows," she said.

"Give me a break. I've never done this before," I said.

She giggled, but tears welled in her eyes. I didn't want to do anything but run somewhere, crouch into a ball, and think about my father, or rather the ghost of the father I had, the one inexact to me now, the one who was trying to tell me that he had died long before. I wanted to tell him I forgave him, that maybe someone could save him from being a ghost if he'd let us peer straight at him and remind him that he was still here, with us. I longed for my mother, to explain to her that I hadn't had the chance to contemplate how demanding it must have been to live with a man who worshipped the air, who *was* air. And that it took a lot of courage, especially when I was angry at her running off, not to blurt the secret that my father must have asked her never to betray.

"Come with me," I whispered to Claudia. I took her hand and hailed a cab and directed the driver to take us to the abyss with the jellyfish. We stood as the wind picked up out of the ocean and blew thick and white around us. I held her hand, and we didn't speak as we watched the heads of the jellyfish, delicate as silk parachutes, otherworldly, present their domes on the surface of the water. Claudia leaned her head on my shoulder, and I smoothed her hair. I kissed her scalp and pretended to be my half-brother, who had belonged here and refused to leave; I pretended he had brought a woman here to show her the holy sights. He must have visited here often, hopeful, waiting, as we do on the edge of the elements, but for who could say what? I wanted to catch him in the reflection of the sun on the water or riding on the foam, some portrait as clear as the one I now carried in my shirt pocket. What was I waiting for? Did Claudia come here calling for her dead husband? Did Carlos come here and call for his son not to throw himself off the cliff? The muscles in my face betrayed me, and I was ready to cry.

She put her arms around my shoulders, and as I drew her closer, I relaxed into an irresolvable state. The world was a place where my mother could walk through my father's door at any moment, where a brother could appear out of thin air, where someone I'd never met before could save me, or I could save him or her. There were endless chances to save someone. I pressed my face against Claudia's, and said, "You lost a young man, too. You hardly had a chance to know him, but his ghost keeps returning and you'll never be free of him. I'm sorry I didn't see that right away." I kissed her nose, her eyelids, her ears, her mouth. I discerned the ruined aspect of the man who'd gone out to save the children in the trees from the bull, and I like to think that red and dripping face forgives me, though it spells out in blood, "You'll see me wavering before you when you least expect it, reminding you to guard and protect whomever and whatever you can."

For now that was Claudia. We made love by the ocean, hidden by some bushes. For several minutes her distant expression told me that she was pretending I was someone else, but I wasn't offended; then it told me that she was truly with me. We laughed about the scene in the church. Darkness was falling. We huddled together under my jacket, with my half-brother against my chest. When she told me, as the moonlight arrived, that everyone had a row of vegetables on my grandfather's land, and would continue to have one even after I named Tia Mafalda's successor, I asked then why in God's name were passions running so high.

"One of us wants to be chosen," she said.

They had enlarged my lawyer father into a judge in a foreign land, with the power to confer a recognition that would say, "You; you are the child of my house. Gaze upon me, and claim what is yours."

"I can't be alone tonight," said Claudia. "Stay with me."

I did. We were still together as the mists slashed in at dawn and a crowd approached the seawall, talking and drinking coffee and eating bread. We were hungry, and they greeted us and shared their food. They were Sebastianites, assembling for the arrival of the lost king. They sat down and checked the shifting, clouded air for the visage that would come to their rescue. Claudia's hand lay over mine. The mist felt good on our skin. Like the cargo cults of the past waiting for the dropping of magical goods out of the airplanes, we sat poised as well, this time for the appearance of a dream. A man offered me some wine, and I let Claudia have some and then I took a sip. An old-timer entertained us with bad juggling, and we groaned. No one seriously expected a vision; everyone was there because hope is lovely. Hope is the most supreme form of defiance. We must learn the comforts of haziness and be at rest beneath veils of fog. We will believe and not believe in the dead and the living king, and though his approach would bring us pleasure, so does his absence present us with an excuse for a party.

If I were patient enough for the mists to shift just right to obscure that tree in the distance, I could climb it and stretch out my arms, and they'd mistake me for Sebastião. From the strength of their trust I could fly where I wanted; I could go to you, and you could tell me who you are and what glories you've seen, and if you are alone, you can impart to me truthfully how you feel to be abandoned; and if you would do me the exquisite kindness, then, of allowing me to read your face, and all that is borne in your eyes.

MATH
BENDING
UNTO
ANGELS

Line + parabola = Clara standing, then bending to put on her shoes.

))) (((§ was Clara listening to a song only once, and then knowing perfectly how to sing it.

| | was Helio walking with her before they joined hands: $| - |$.

If $| \square$ was Clara in front of a window, then $| \square \times 7 = x$, x being unknown, was Clara throughout a week, with her private thoughts. Sometimes they seemed to carry her far away, which terrified him, ($H^{x!x}$). He was almost thirty years older than Clara, and like all widowers he was nervous that God would decide he was accustomed to anguish and could bear more. His head filled every pause and empty space with geometry and formulas, as if his wishing hard enough would bring forth shapes that would amuse her, and with a logic that would keep her his. To stay young and protect her, he enrolled in a karate class but was overcome by the first lesson: Bowing is urged so that the head is not continually held higher than the heart. He loved this idea to the point that he bowed constantly during each set, even when it was dangerous. He kept getting thrown. One night the sensei handed him his glasses and said he was a nice man but he had to leave.

⊕; or Clara ($\int\int\int$ her long brown hair), joining him in the bathtub and sponging down his bruised skin.

When he had to go work at his dental clinic, so intense were his thoughts of her that his hands shook, making him afraid of hurting people's gums. In his garden he was trying to graft some of his dental tools to sugar cane, to allow him to probe the teeth of patients more sweetly. But the grafts were not taking. Hard silver stalks dissolved into sugar the moment they poked out of the ground, before they could be picked.

He frowned at them. Clara sat watching, and began to sing. Her voice! Her voice! The wind told stories to her and she opened her mouth and retold everything in music, and it made him too happy to breathe right. *Faraway I shall search for thee,/High, wide* . . . her notes fell around her feet and around him, * * *, seeds.

He was going to kick himself. Clara! Clara would fix these awful dental tools! He ran into the house for the photos of the two of them at the fair. They were grinning. Clara with him at a fair— there was heaven. After roughing up the edges of the photos, he tied them to some dental instruments and packed them into the moist ground. Clara applauded and took off her sandals to slap their soles against a rock to harmonize her laughter. He was going to raise metal hooks that instead of having patients flinch would have them dreaming of hay and fair games and angels.

Because she was an angel.

An angel, that was the word he had been waiting to be bestowed on him for the last three years, since the hour of meeting her. An angel, angel; he could not sleep that night, overwhelmed with the notion of her being an angel, and was seized with the hope that he could give her everything. He rose out of bed. At the window he saw pieces of moon caught like manna in the trees. Above that, he pictured a choir of Claras in sheer dresses. | ↑ ♀: Helio at the window with his calculations reaching an apex inside him. All math, all now, would be in the service of computing how to give an angel what she needed. He could not return Clara's dead parents to her, but when he found her staring distantly, he could point her toward the completeness that angels dwelled in, and so bring her back to herself.

The army of Claras above was chanting: O O O

Whole notes. Music! Sometimes he was as dense as enamel! Angels needed music! He would convert their home into giant harps, bigger than anyone could imagine, and he felt so buoyed by his plans that he found himself in the sky with the choir. He reached out and lifted an angel's skirt while climbing onto her, her breasts in his hands as he kissed her neck.

Turning around, he saw Clara looking curiously at him. Embarrassed, he folded his arms across his chest, then wanted to travel instantly the few hours it would take to get to the Pacific, where they could run up and down on the beach. Instead they stood naked at the window. She did not ask what he was doing or thinking. She ran her hand down the curve of his back, and he lifted her onto him. Parallel lines joined as one; sinking into each other.

$$| \, | \Rightarrow |, \text{ and again } | \, | \Rightarrow |$$

It was scary if she thought about it. What did being an angel mean anyhow and what was this about building harps, but she would wait and see. He always had to be arranging something or fixing it anyway . . . last night making love with her feet off the earth and around him, that was enough of being an angel but maybe more was not going to hurt. . . . This morning she made love to him on the kitchen table, and it was great that for an hour later some crumbs were still stuck to her back because that was proof that she was loved. That was important because when a person was not there anymore how did you stop from saying Love me, even when you are gone, do you love me, did you. . . . Helio read to her sometimes and words on a page looked like black hairs on a clean white sheet, and that was why reading reminded her of love. . . . She whip-kicked. She wished she could do butterfly, legs going up and down together, but that looked amazing and impossible. The grasses swayed beneath her, . . . swimming was incredible, like changing death into something without a body, weightless. She used to be afraid of water because back home in the Azores her father got lost at sea. Helio said go into it, go right into what you fear and then everything about it is yours, your father loved the water and drowned in what he loved. So she swam in the lake like this every morning and when she . . . was that a fish? . . . climbed onto shore her skin would shout up in dots and she would tremble. That was love also. Helio would be waiting, he was the part of her heart healed over, he should stop thinking so much because it worried her it would wear him out, thinking too much cut life up into little pieces like meat for a toothless person, and . . . Look! A necklace buried halfway over there in the silt. Maybe it belonged to a noblewoman who was . . . kidnapped. No, murdered, lost forever, here in this lake! Her ghost wandered . . .

Clara surfaced. He approached, holding a towel to warm her.

They hung strings throughout the house, using thumbtacks to fasten the ends to a wall or to the furniture. Some strings filled doorways in straight waterfalls and had to be stretched into diamonds before a person could enter a room. The bedroom was a taut jungle slanting down from the ceiling. Clara could reach up anywhere and clutch at stringed air and surround the two of them with music, which occasionally made Helio go out of his head and dash around, but strings caught his body and played in large twangs that made her giggle.

"Don't stop," he pleaded. "Don't stop for me. Do you know any *fados?*" These were the Portuguese songs of fate, a kind of possession by love and sadness that must start below the diaphragm and reverberate in the throat before leaving the singer's body.

"I know a few. My mother used to sing them." She also could play and sing some of the happier *fados*, the kind called *fados corridos*, or running *fados*, because the melody could not be bothered to stay contented in one place for very long.

He settled against white webs as she plucked the bedroom harp. She made his geometry real and alive, not stuck in his thoughts! Real and alive, and *singing*. He touched himself all over, especially the storehouse of his chest, to feel his arteries pulsating inside himself during her concerts. He would not survive if he kept this theirs alone. People everywhere needed a formula for creating angels. As Clara sang, he wrote:

$$\left(\frac{W}{music}\right) + \left(\frac{?}{?}\right) + \left(\frac{?}{?}\right) = angel$$

W = Witten's string theory: The universe is composed of countless wriggling strings, some no bigger than particles, others tremendous. They are the building materials of everything.

Thank you, Witten! Where was Witten? Did he need a dental

check-up? Helio would pour Miracle-Gro on his grafts and use the sweetened fair-tools on Witten, for free.

She knitted cat's-cradles in the harps. It was easy for her to fix hammocks for them right below the ceiling, but more difficult to teach Helio how to climb string ladders and swing across a room to get to her. They brought food up into the harps and ate there, and in a short while they were completely living suspended. Being off the ground so much was like swimming, except that it was in the air. Setting up the harps was happiness, but being subject to their laws was joy; joy took happiness and made it sway.

Helio was nervous when the strings stretched and sagged. The shortest distance between two points was no longer a simple line; how could he kid himself? Because curved objects changed all measurements into curves. He reminded himself, uneasily, of Einstein's warning that the greater the degree of certainty in mathematics, the less it had to do with reality.

Joy was non-Euclidean.

Joy demanded curves, never the head over the heart.

Whatever joy held, it promised unending surprise.

None of that told him what to put instead of the second set of question marks in his formula.

One day while examining a patient, Joey Daniels, Helio grew very fearful to observe that everyone has upper and lower teeth shaped as $U + U$. People walked around with these unions of half-circles clamped together, never forming an infinite circle. Joey bit him, and Helio jumped.

When Clara bandaged Helio's thumb, she discovered that the throbbing in it, purple, was speaking to her. She could suddenly hear every shade of purple around her. Some were chanting quietly, and some were loud. The satchel of lavender in her drawer was gossiping about her nightgowns. The vase of lilacs, tied up with strings and hanging halfway between the ceiling and floor in the kitchen, was chattering about missing the ground. The purple of Helio's thumb was in tempo with the beat of his heart, throwing its own *fado* at her.

"Shh," she said, kissing it.

"I cannot," said the purple.

"Why not?" she said.

"What?" said Helio.

"I'm hearing purple everywhere," she explained to him.

"I am the color of grief," said the purple. "Don't you remember that your mother became purple with sorrow after your father drowned?"

After wrapping Helio's thumb and muffling what it was saying to her, Clara said she was tired. But rest did not come. The lilacs were murmuring as she lay awake next to Helio in their hammocks, and in the morning the violet sky said, "While everyone sleeps, there is a battle between light and dark, and the night is so fierce that the dawn arrives bruised, the color you see before you. Did you think that if you hid away here in California, your mother's lamentations would never find you?"

When Helio awoke and saw Clara staring upward, and she said she would never sleep at peace again because night was purple upon purple, the color of the deepest part of the sea, he said: Go to what you fear. Praise the night. Claim the night. Angels are that strong.

He demolished the roof, and they wore the night as a cape. When she felt the fierceness in the mysteries outside their house, when the struggles between night and day caused the day to puncture itself on the edges of the stars, she curled up near Helio and plucked at a harp string. It was not so bad to have knocked out the roof. Around her, Helio drew shelter and song:

////// \\\\\ §♪§

Music belongs to angels, but flight does also. That would be the logical next step. He convinced her that with the air drafts floating in and out through the open roof, she could walk on the strings, and that would teach her which drafts had a velocity that would lift her.

"I'll need a parasol, Helio," she said.

"Those are only for show. They don't have anything to do with balance. Make the air your home."

"Parasols are nice," she said. "Please."

"Fly."

"Catch me if I fall."

"Go. Keep your eyes straight ahead, and don't think about anything else. Fly."

"I want a parasol."

He bought her a parasol. Over the passing weeks, while she practiced, he visited the studio of a glassblower and taught himself how to regulate the flames and the equipment as he blew glass tubes into the size of beams, emptying his lungs. His efforts made him light-headed. At home he hung the glass beams to allow her to walk not only on the harp strings, but on the living remains of everything inside him, and he wrote:

$$a = \text{all of a person's inner air}$$

$$V^c = \text{velocity} + \text{currents of air that are willing}$$

$$\left(\frac{W}{music} \right) + \left(\frac{a/V^c}{flight} \right) + \left(\frac{?}{?} \right) = \text{angel}$$

His breath stayed warm in the glass, now that was a miracle. She expected the tubes to be cold but they were not. . . . No matter what he said, a parasol *was* nice. Pretending to be a tightrope-walker was fun, who cared about angels . . . sequins. She liked shiny ones. The crowd going "Huuu!" thinking she might slip, and "Uhh, ohh," when she stayed up. . . . In a circus, people traveled to many countries . . . and tigers. Curries. Different cities, and . . . goodness! She almost fell but then walking on the breath of him made her fly again. He was rocking on some strings down below, writing numbers on papers, his face still purple from an afternoon of taking out his air for her . . . cities like Singapore with wild animals, she hoped. This business of the roof gone was good, it put sun on her face.

"My blood is flying as high as it can," said the purple in his face to her.

"Calm down," she sang to it.

"I cannot," said the purple.

"You must. For your health. Shall I tell you a story? There once was a young girl who loved a dentist, so much it hurt, and . . ."

"There once was a young angel, you mean," said Helio, "and if you'll forgive me for saying so, he was more than just a dentist."

"Are you going to let me tell it my way or not?" said Clara.

"Sorry. Go on."

"There once was a young girl who loved a grafter, a scientist, so much that it hurt, and she wondered what she had done to deserve what he gave her."

"You don't need to do anything," his blood said to her fervently.

"That's just it. I do need to do something," she said. "Up to now what have I done? I haven't done anything."

"Angel," said the purple blood. "Angel, angel . . . ," and it shouted down anything else she might have to say. Because it could not say aloud that after joy there comes the fright of ecstasy. What had he started? He should have guessed that prying open the door to heaven even a little might be blinding. Hadn't the poet Rainer Maria Rilke said that every angel was terrible? Not that Clara was terrible, never that; it was only that beauty, when allowed to thrive, was not of this world, and therefore it burned like a fleck of sun. It was easier to be poetic about fire when one's hand was not held in it. (That old churchman Meister Eckhardt had warned that God was too brilliant to behold, and therefore the angels served as His reflectors, much as the moon offers its dull shield to sunlight.) O what had he done? What would follow?

Terrified, he decided to pursue ordinary things rather than the third set of question marks in his equation. He drove to the store to buy some new T-shirts. But his car threatened to overheat on the road, he took several wrong turns, and he was shaking by the time he found a parking space. People behind him honked as he backed out and drove forward in the space several times to align his car properly. In the men's department, the array of shirts was bewildering, and he refused to consider one with anything written on it. Standing for a long time holding a package of plain ones that were actually undershirts, he wondered if it would be humiliating to wear them with nothing else. When a clerk asked if he needed help, he threw down the package and ran.

At the lunch counter in the store, he ordered a bowl of soup and a soda. That was pleasant. Not the soup, which was thin and oily, but the sense that a person could sit for a while with other people on these stools covered with a cheery yellow plastic. A little girl was perched next to him, with her mother on the stool next to hers. He flattened his red-and-white striped straw, tied it into a bow, and set it in the girl's hair. She laughed and reached up to pat it.

Her mother knocked it off with one swipe of her hand. "That was in *his mouth*," she hissed, glaring over the child's head at Helio.

"O, I didn't mean to upset you." His hand covered the lower half of his face, and his mustache bristled in horror. His gold-rimmed glasses slipped down his nose. Should he offer to pay for the girl's lunch? He fumbled around and took a few dollars out of his wallet. The bow lay in the gummy dirt on the floor. "Here," he said to the girl, gesturing vaguely with the money.

The mother's face contracted with disgust.

He stuffed the money back into his wallet and prepared to flee, although he did not get more than a few strides away before the waitress yelled, "Hey! That'll be three-fifty for the soup!"

"Certainly. Forgive me!" he said. Everyone was staring. His mind blanked out in the panic of not knowing how to calculate the proper tip. He threw a ten-dollar bill on the counter and escaped, his legs wobbling.

He had to walk up and down every row in the parking lot to find his car, and he was quaking by the time he did. Resting his head on the wheel to collect himself, he tried to wish himself back where he belonged.

Along his return, rain began falling; it would be falling through their open roof. He stared through the windshield, angry at himself. Why had he torn away their ceiling? Did he think winter was not going to come? Clara would be drenched, and the harps would be soaked! What a mess! Another one of his bright ideas!

He arrived home expecting to find her miserable and huddled in a corner, but she was dancing around the room that was a box of rain opened toward the sky. Water dripped from her hair and coursed off her dress. She was singing patches of songs, jumping from one lyric to another.

"Maybe angels aren't flying things with harps!" she cried. "Maybe they're this!" She held out her hands so that the water formed leaping ponds in her palms.

"They're rain?" he asked. Angels are rain? Simple rain? Drops like tiny fingers tapped the thinning black hair on his scalp.

"Water that can be held and not held!" she said, and laughed. She was talking like him.

He fought through the soggy harp strings to get to his desk, took out his papers, and arranged them where the rain could erase what was on them. His work smudged and went cryptic and swam away as he stood there a moment, bidding it farewell. What good were his additions and figures? + + +, arranged like headstones in a graveyard. Just this easily, something could happen or a person could speak, and with one definition could change a lifetime of work, to remind everyone that everything was always a matter of redefining, letting go, starting over. He set out glasses of red wine, and the rain-angels must have enjoyed his homage to their power over him, because the wine soon disappeared and the glasses were emptied and running over with clear rain. Drunk and victorious, the angels were stomping up and down in the glasses. Clara was singing water music.

Rain lived invisible in the sky, in the heavens that were angelically swollen, whether or not it was stormy. That was the final component of the equation. Angels were invisible. They took shape by going here and there. He tried not to break apart as Clara, wet with rain, flung off her clothes and came to sit in his lap, her face glorious. Hugging her richly, he could only hope that with him her fears had somewhat ended. Now he had to go himself to what he feared the most, which was the promise of this, that she might be invisible and disappear from him. He could not finish telling her that soon she would leave him. Angels ride high. They must invent their own journeys, especially when they are young. They go into the water that killed their fathers, and live in the rainlike tears of their grieving mothers, and fear nothing. Every day spent with an angel before the weather shifts, every hour until then is blessed.

In the garden he checked how the rain was treating the dental tools grafted to the photo from the fair. The heads of the instruments were sprouting with the metal hay-colored and malleable. A harvest might be ready soon. Alongside this crop he grafted a potato to a dictionary, in order that a root could exist wherein every combination of words was within reach, since he did not know how to express what he felt.

Another year passed. Helio was watchful. Sometimes the days were dry, and sometimes there was rain.

Then one day when Clara was alone in the garden, a purple crocus said to her, "Look! Come closer, angel."

She did. "There's nothing."

"Look more closely."

"Nothing."

"Stop being a coward and open your eyes," said the purple.

She saw a lizard using camouflage to hide on a brown twig. "So?" she said.

The purple was getting exasperated. "So scrape off some of its chromatophores and rub them on your skin. There's dew on them, and next time a shower hits, you'll be able to change into rain. You'll get to be invisible and watery, and then you'll rise up and travel with the weather."

"Travel?" she said.

"Travel," said the purple.

She caught the lizard and scraped off some of its scales. She gazed at them trapped under her fingernail. Playing camouflage made her feel like an inventor, like Helio. . . . Should she ask him first? But here was a chance for her to do something herself. The crocuses were bossy. . . . She had heard that if a person flew very early into a city, there was gold trim on the buildings. In San Francisco, the clouds rolled over the homes in bands like white oceans. . . . In China, the buildings were pointed up, like arrows. . . . O and the Azores, she could visit where she had been born and meet people and collect more and more stories and live by singing . . .

She released the lizard and rubbed the scales on her skin, over her face and arms and legs and inside her shift, and went to tell Helio what she had discovered.

/// was Clara running toward the hammock where he was.

√ was Clara with her head bent back, informing him that she knew the final step in how to realize herself as an angel. She recited everything that she had heard and done in the garden. But somehow she did not connect it yet to leaving him, he could see that. Nestling the book he had been reading into a tangle of strings, climbing out of the hammock to come down and face her, his temples were pounding, although he appeared calm. The day he had been dreading was here. He had not known how it would arrive, but he knew he would recognize it when it did. It would require the last of his strength to impress upon her that she must rise invisibly, as angels do.

He stood before her. Now that she had the means of going away, the suspense of waiting for the next rain to envelop and carry her in camouflage from him would be more than he could stand. If this had to take place, let it be at once. It is a well-known truth that rain will fall after a battle; it is the air's reaction to the heat and spectacle of conflict. It is God washing away what is appalling. If Helio started an argument with Clara, the surprise in the air would cause the terrible forces to collide. Rain would come. Torrents would cascade into their home.

He inhaled. "A lizard teaching you something! What a stupid idea!"

She stared at him, shocked. He had never said anything cross with her, nothing impatient. "It isn't," she said.

"Idiotic!"

"Helio, I'm only—"

"Living in fantasyland." He turned his face aside.

"Helio." She put a hand on his arm, and he thrust it off.

"Leave me alone! Go away!"

A light rain misted over them. Unannounced, it had answered his summons.

"You don't mean it," she whispered.

"I—" He stopped. This was too hard. He was not ready to lose her. His body felt as if he had been running for miles. But as he prepared to take it all back, the mist was intensifying into a drizzle, and as he reached toward her the scales with their camouflage powers were already forcing her skin to melt. She was pale, and he tried to grasp her but could not. The drops were pulling her upward. As she left the floor and the specter of her rose through the strings, he shouted, "Don't worry! It isn't colder as you go higher, the way everyone thinks! The heat rises into the stratosphere! It'll be warm for you!" He threw himself onto a ladder of strings and began frantically climbing.

"Helio!"

The rain was falling full force. Pain chewed at his ligaments. He commanded his hands to grasp higher strings, but he was not quick enough to catch up with her. He could not stand this, could not—the last spark of logic left to him was Einstein's law of photochemistry: one quantum of light—in this case, Clara—can cause a direct photochemical change in exactly one molecule of matter. He would remain that corporal molecule, but wherever she went he would be changed by the light of her; where she was he would therefore be an angel too.

As he looked up and saw the fading outline of her, growing more indistinct as it went toward the pressures that would transport her across valleys and cities, to dapple rivers and be drunk by the earth and then set free again and again—Clara paler, leaving— he burst out weeping, "O, of course I don't mean it! I can't! You're my whole world!"

"Come with me!" she shrieked.

The rain was soaking him. He held out his hands to collect the storm and call it an angel, as she had taught him to do. This would be how he would hold her for the rest of his life.

She was ascending through the open ceiling. "You know how to be an angel, you figured it out," she screamed. "Come with me!"

But he needed to be flesh remembering her flesh. "People aren't angels enough. Tell everyone what's possible," he called out. "My love."

She vanished.

Her light, his weight: changed by the light of her. *Where you go I am therefore an angel too.*

He would wait the weeks and months and entire Californian seasons between rainfalls, until he could feel her pouring over him with the shifting and returning weather fronts. She would sweep pounding in through the open roof, reporting back all that she had seen and the young men she loved, none as purely as him, but that was what flying over the land of possibilities meant—and he would hold out his arms to the rain, and listen to her tales of purple talk, and beg her to sing, and she would ask what was his heart's desire now that the wide world out there was hers, and he would close his eyes and shake his head as the water washed over him and say, *"Only you. Only you."*

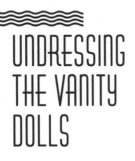

UNDRESSING
THE VANITY
DOLLS

To buy some time, Reginald peered at the doorknocker. His face danced like a gremlin's on the polished surface. He glanced away, and the door creaked as he opened it and spilled the smell of a sickroom, like a brew of oranges and pesticides, into the street. Professor Dias should be more careful about locking up. But then his whole life had been a studious approach to carelessness, carefreeness, though now, of course, very little of that mattered. Reginald paused in the dark living room, with its furniture pushed back against the walls, as if nothing had changed since the days of Dias's parties for his students. There was the rolltop desk with its maple ribs and the teakwood elephant tables from Brazil that displayed vases of asphodels. Reginald almost smiled. He never told anyone how well he could catalogue flowers. Apparently Dias continued to have a florist deliver bouquets every day. Reginald remembered admiring how unerringly these deliveries went on, even when Dias was off on one of his trips. Adventures, he called them. Student house sitters (often it had been Reginald) reported that a parade of exotic plants— branches of currants, motherwort, cockscombs—arrived. Dias's counsel was that a person should commit to heart the names of the most attractive ones. This possession of names, he argued, was borrowed from the opening act of Eden, when the first man and woman had named what surrounded them; this enabled them to roam the earth and speak with authority to what was on it.

The rug, gold and scarlet, was worn into a precious antique rather than a threadbare relic. The velvet curtains were old but still thick, which had always made the house seem like an extension out from a chamber. Despite everything, despite what Alicia had told him years ago, Reginald found it hard to stop thinking of Dias as *his*, Reginald's, professor, though twenty years had passed since Dias's botany classes. Or since Reginald began not answering Dias's letters or phone messages, until yesterday's call. Reginald had met Alicia in Dias's class. He had often listened to music here—Benny Goodman, Stravinsky, zarzuelas, tarantellas, Portuguese *fados*, the songs about fate and longing—until after midnight in this house when everyone, especially Dias, was drunk. Dias favored the Coimbra-style *fados*, the kind sung by men. At the University of Coimbra in Portugal, the young men went about in black robes that they ripped whenever they had a romantic conquest. Handsome fellows, rushing about in their proud tatters! Reginald should have seen his professor's fondness for their singing as indicative of what was to come. As it was, Dias needed hardly any persuasion to dance flamenco in this living room as his students, particularly the female ones, applauded. His wife went back to Madeira at some point and never returned.

Reginald could feel Dias in the bedroom at the back of the house and tried to picture what he might look like after all this time. Over the doorway was the faded, hand-lettered placard of one of Dias's works:

Listen for the nightingale that presses its breast against the
    thorns of the rose,
That the song might be more beautiful.
Chant to me that song, and the song made of your
    dedication to that song.

It had been posted behind the lectern in his classroom, and even now Reginald did not have to see it to be able to recite every word from memory. Dias's lectures were equally florid, and he surrounded himself with flowers and gracious antiques, but he could also be flat-toned. Blunt. Possessed of chummy language. It had taken Reginald a while to listen past the flowers, just as it took time to realize that some men who taught the same thing for too long used whatever lyricism was at their means to hydrate their weariness and seduce young women. Dias had pressed plenty to his breast, but when had it ever been a thorn? But twenty years ago, Reginald had memorized what he was told to know.

He also received more invitations to lunch than any other student in Dias's entire tenure at the university, for a good reason. Reginald's father was an Englishman who had run an embroidery shop on the island of Madeira, southeast from the Azores, and Reginald's mother had been a Madeirense who consented to quit embroidering and live, temporarily, in a big whitewashed home with a terra-cotta roof, overlooking a sheer rock face. Legend had it that Madeira was where the golden apples grew that Hercules sought as one of his labors, but she glared over the wild fennel and jacaranda trees and became restless. Reginald's father moved her to the East Bay area of San Francisco, where Reginald was born. Eduardo Dias, though he grew up in Madeira, did not meet Reginald's parents until their son was one of his most promising botany students at Berkeley. Dias had not left the island because he was bored—he was never bored—but to find a larger audience.

Madeira was the Portuguese word for wood, and the island's dense forests were supposed to have burned in the sea for seven years. The trees survived, petrified. It was an image fiery, glamorous, and faraway for Reginald, whose mother could only love her native land if she missed it. That was why meeting Dias had been like a dream. As they drank beer in the Golden Bear Faculty Club, he entertained Reginald with stories of the homeland that Reginald had been cheated of; of the wicker carts on wooden runners that tourists climbed into, to be driven clattering down steep cobbled streets, or of that history of fire that survived in the brightness of the banana plants, hibiscus, and gardenias. The Madeirense could carry astonishingly heavy burdens up the hill-sides. The people spread carpets made of flowers throughout the streets on festival days, patterns constructed from ground-up petals. The existence of flower carpets was in some ways the finest detail. To turn the very ground into floral pictures!

All this was more luxuriant than anything Reginald met with in the suburbs, and he crawled gladly under Dias's wing. Right out of college, Reginald saved enough to marry Alicia and take her to Madeira for their honeymoon, and more than remarking on what they saw, they talked beneath the blooms of the torch lamps at the cafés on the black-sand beaches of Funchal about how accurate Eduardo Dias had been in describing everything, right down to the delicacy of the azaleas.

A Chinese porcelain umbrella stand was propping open the hallway door. A nasty thought entered Reginald's head: Which flower is tear like, Professor? For you, I mean. Not me. A Venus fly-trap, a carnivore?

Reginald entered the bedroom, which was warm as a hot-house. He looked at his professor lying in bed, and was relieved that he was sleeping, because it gave Reginald time to adjust to what the last two decades had done. The usual signs of aging were there, the sparse white hair and neck creases, though Dias had the same high forehead, the same features that looked carved instead of molded like everyone else's, but there were also purple bulges of marbleized blood beneath the surface of his face, proof that a person could be forced to wear the truth on his skin. *Epochs of drinking,* the veins were shouting, and so was the broken hip that had him laid up in order for the cirrhosis to finish killing him.

Reginald tried to name what he was feeling, but all he could think to call it was an urgent wondering. Either the great Eduardo Dias had summoned him, like the rest of the favorite students from the past, for an official good-bye, or Dias was going to tell him the truth, maybe apologize. Reginald would settle for finally hearing what had transpired between Alicia and Dias, did you, didn't you, the end. To this day, she refused to say if she had slept with Dias or not. Reginald's marriage to Alicia was redolent with what was withheld, which made it an ordinary, garden-variety union. That was what secrets could do, and he resented their potency more than some distant unfaithfulness. He and Alicia had separated five times over the years, but even to that kind of definition they could not hold themselves.

He coughed, attempting to make Dias fight through the soporific effects of the perfume from the bouquets filling the room. The heads of the flowers were studiously bowed, and the stems seemed to float like interstices of folded air. Reginald read some of the delivery cards. Most of them were from women, although Dias was over sixty-five.

Next to the trophies from amateur dance contests stuck on the shelves was a collection of vanity dolls. Reginald was startled. His mother's aunt had been a nun in Madeira, in Curral das Freiras, a crater-like valley with a convent that had been built to be safe from pirates, and he knew what the dolls were for: people used them to displace vain desires. If a nun, or any devout person, painted a ballgown onto a doll and gave it new earrings, the doll absorbed her wish to have those things. A doll dressed as a sailor could cure a travel bug, and one painted with flowers could relieve someone of carnal aches. What was Eduardo doing with vanity dolls? In one way, it made sense. They were curios, caked with the ancient, flung-off passions of women. Nice little trophies. Only they were so heavily painted, with layers of flowers and outfits, that they looked shrouded.

"Sit down," came the greeting from the bed.

Reginald turned to see Professor Dias wincing as he tried to sit up. Reginald did not go to assist him, but he sat as he had been told.

"Professor," he said. *Name the names of what is before you, if you are unclear. Naming contains the inherent description.* He loosened his tie; why had he worn a tie?

"You've gotten old, Reg," laughed Dias hoarsely. If he felt embarrassed at how he looked, he was doing a good job of hiding it. "Life as an astrologer been rough on you, eh?"

"It's Reginald. I go by Reginald now. And that's astronomer."

"I know it, for the love of God," said Dias. "Relax. What I don't know is how you propose to get me out of here."

"Sir?"

"Quit the sir stuff. Everyone who comes to see me is a weakling. Since you weren't calling me, I had to call you. I had to guess if you'd be right for this job. You're still pretty strapping, I see. You work out with weights, Reg? I do." He pressed both his fists upward, raising an invisible bar. "Why are you sitting there? I said get me out of here."

"I heard you have a broken hip, sir."

"I know what I have and don't have, Reg, and I don't think my cast weighs so much you can't offer some assistance. There's a red tide coming in tonight, and I have to get to the beach."

"The closest beach is over an hour away, and I don't know what a red tide is."

"All the more reason," said Dias impatiently, "for you to take me there."

"Don't you have a nurse to come help you?"

"Yes, but she's a weakling, and you don't see her here right now, do you."

Reginald leaned back to keep from collapsing in a rage. Not a single question asking how he was, nothing to reconcile the long silence. Nothing about Alicia; Reginald had expected some sly question about her. Or did Dias not care about her anymore? That seemed like the worst insult of all. As the professor threw his bare legs out from under the covers, they both knew that Reginald would not allow his teacher to sprawl on the ground.

Tell me if you can, ladies and gentlemen, the language of the flowers. Don't you believe they have one? What if I told you that while the base of the lotus concerns itself with eloquence, its flower speaks of estrangement? Can you fathom how the two of them must live together? You must learn to listen! To the falsehoods of the yellow lily, and the innocent claims of the white lily; to what you mean by giving someone a pineapple, which asserts: "You are perfect." Do not put saffron in a soup, unless you wish to declare that your fondest days are behind you. Very sad for me; home in Madeira we put saffron and mint in the fish soup. At least mint is all about virtue. Go to the sycamore when you are consumed by curiosity. I cannot report much about the sycamores, because when I am curious about something I find out what I need, just as I keep looking for the person who can talk this language with me. Never bring me a fruitcake at Christmas. Citron is about prettiness that is unpleasant. I once gave a young lady a Japan rose, which means . . . ? Aha, none of you know either! The flower was telling her "good looks are your only blessing," and no one got the joke but me.

Reginald had discarded all the tapes of Dias's lectures, but that had not erased them from memory. He smelled Dias's unwashed hair as he helped him put on some trousers with the outer seam of one leg completely split. The professor's torso oozed out of the white clay pot of the cast. Reginald took two belts off the bed table and used them to fasten the open trouser leg. The cast was heavy and kept knocking into Reginald as he let Dias lean on him. A vanity doll with daisies over her eyes stared at them. Before they hobbled from the room, Reginald noticed a lunch tray with a pear core: affection. From the nurse? *Pears! Pairings—don't you get it? Ladies and gentlemen, the problem is that you're too serious! Look at you! Serious! Don't you think plants have a sense of humor? Have a pear for lunch, then go wink at someone!*

At the shoreline, Reginald put Dias slightly out of reach of the foam turning to exploding lace on the sand. The air was cooling down, into evening. Dias lay on his side, his flannel shirt already damp. Reginald followed his professor's gaze out to a vibrant blue flow that was moving in a ribbon across a current toward them, out of some gash in the sea, iridescent. The neon splendor rode along slowly, then boomed, sparking blue, on the surf. Though he went out many times to walk alone at night, though he was a fair sailor, Reginald had never seen anything like this. A red tide? Why was it blue?

"Phosphorescent animals," said Reginald. "Correct?"

"Very good, Reginald," said Dias.

Reginald hesitated. "All right then. I give up. Why is it called a red tide when it is obviously blue?"

Dias's elbow had a patch of wet sand as he lifted his arm to point. "The bodies of the dead animals are red, but their phosphorescent organ makes them glow blue at night. Did you know that navigators used them to read their maps, when the oil or kerosene was gone and the ship was lost in the dark? Sailors dipped their hands into a red tide and then held them over their maps."

"They read by the light of a red tide?" asked Reginald.

"Yes. Go on." Dias gestured toward the waves.

Reginald took off his shoes and rolled the cuffs of his trousers.

The waves were subdued and the tide low enough to permit him to wade in until he could put his arms into the water. He wanted the red-blue animals past his elbows and did not bother to remove his coat. He held his arms steady and submerged as the blue glow coursed around him. When he stood, his arms and the part of his chest that had been splashed were vibrant for scarcely a second, and then the brilliance vanished. He shivered. But how strange and wonderful to see this light show on the water! Once again, Dias knew the best secrets. He had the strangest way of making people need to give something in return.

As Reginald stepped from the sea, he asked, "May I explain how to read the stars?"

He heard himself talking about the stars appearing solid, when they were nothing more than hot gases. He jumped to the Age of Discovery—Dias had taught him about Magalhães, or Magellan, and the other Portuguese explorers—but what was the earth, compared to what they were finding out then about the stars? Think of Copernicus, suggesting that the world as everyone knew it, terra firma, was not the center of the universe. That meant no one could profess himself at the center of the universe either, since he revolved in something bigger. Reginald heard himself mention that the moons around each planet performed a trackable ballet, and that our galaxy was funny. Why else would it drape itself with constellations of punished captives, like Cassiopeia over there in the north sky, whose five brightest stars formed not a lovely woman but a chair, where she was confined by Neptune for boasting of her beauty?

Dias was listening and rolled over to lie on his back. But living with Alicia had versed Reginald in speaking expansively while deliberating on something removed. He lost his desire to be giving a lecture at the beach; he wanted to settle the matter of Alicia. How long he had been in the dark—since a few weeks after returning with her from their honeymoon in Madeira. Before he had developed the pictures they took, that soon afterward, she told him offhandedly, one night while stuffing a chicken for dinner, that she was sort of in love with Eduardo Dias. Not a day passed in which she failed to think of him. If for some reason life as she recognized it were to change—meaning, Reginald supposed, that he, her new husband, keeled over—she was glad there was someone out there for her.

Out there. The gooseflesh bumps on the chicken disgusted him, and so did the sodden brown mass she was shoving into its cavity. She was not breaking stride with what she was doing, and that ease of speaking of love, or "sort of love," or whatever it was, while preoccupied with a task meant that she could indeed do one thing while being quite lost in another, and that irritated him unspeakably. He tried to control himself. A lot of the women at Berkeley had been infatuated with Dias.

"He had that ability," he said, his voice rising, "to make everyone feel that he, or she, I suppose, was the only other person alive. It's a gift. He was like that with me."

"I was different." She picked up a huge needle and coarse thread to sew up the bird. The fatty yellow flesh took the jabs.

"How were you different? Turn off that water, if you're not using it."

"I am using it. I was just different, that's all."

"Explain."

As she put down the knife and looked at him, an old armor clanked off them and a new vestment took its place, and more vestments on top of that, right then with the smell of chicken skin and the sound of the faucet running. She maintained that if she got a little comfort from thinking of Dias, Reginald should not be petty and bourgeois and whatever else it was that he was, he could hardly recall. He admitted to being problematic about what did and did not matter, if only because he had introduced her to Dias. Had she forgotten that? If she happened to be speaking about a crush, why not say so? If it had been more than that, why was she wounding him at the beginning of their marriage? She replied with some nonsense about Reginald being the one who was determined to reduce everything to sex, which was exactly what would keep her from saying if anything sexual had happened. Besides, she had married Reginald. What did anything else matter? She was only trying to suggest how Dias made (not had made, but made) her feel. And they lived a hundred miles from Berkeley now.

That was how it was left. She worked at a chemist's and came home every night on time. Within the year he quit his job at the arboretum, turned down a position as a research assistant at an agricultural lab, and went back to school, this time at the University of California at Davis, for his astronomy degree. Occasionally the fight was rekindled.

He threw away the letters and postcards that Dias sent him. Him, not Alicia. He was usually the first at the mail, and if it ever possessed Alicia to write to her old mentor, he did not appear to be responding. Reginald bought a phone machine, and after a while Dias quit calling him. Calling *him,* he noted. Sometimes a letter or message included a "say hello to . . . ," but that was the extent of it. It was good when the calls stopped, since the professor's voice made Reginald nostalgic, as if he were in the faculty club, hearing how to make the powerful, sweet madeira wine, or how the men constructed the *levadas,* the channels that brought water off the mountaintops to the villages: an engineering marvel. Thirty-five men died in the process of building it.

In twenty years of marriage, Reginald had slept with seven other women and told Alicia about three of them. She had confessed to two affairs, which might have been none; her men sounded invented, to equalize what they both called his adventures. Even if her others were true, he only cared about Dias. When Reginald asked from time to time, trying to sound casual, if she still thought about the professor, she shrugged and said that certainly she did, and why not?

The call yesterday from Dias had come for Reginald. Alicia did not know where he was right now. He would have to discover how to tell her that Dias was dying.

He lost the thread of what he was saying aloud about the constellations. The ocean air was cold.

"Go on," said Dias. "You were just warming up." Under the moonlight his face was green from the poisons in his liver, but he was grinning. This late, this deep into retirement, he had the strength to rhapsodize and lead others into their own enchantments. He could get his broken body out of bed and take someone to a red tide. Reginald knew then, better than he had ever known how to name it, that vitality was plainly the clothing that sexuality wears, so that it can go out in public. That was what his professor was made of, that was his cloak, his finery.

"I can't go on," said Reginald, rolling down his trouser legs and stuffing his wet feet back into his socks and shoes. "I forget where I was."

"Then take me home, and let's have a drink." His white hair was as glistening as silk fresh out of worms from mulberry trees. (Dark mulberries said, "I cannot survive you.") Dias had always seemed old, even back then, when he had been as old as Reginald was now, but his age these days seemed the wrong draping over who he was. An unfair draping.

"I'll take you back," said Reginald.

"For a drink. Let's have a goddamn drink, man."

"I'll put you down to rest," said Reginald, his voice subdued.

"Aren't you listening? I pride myself in keeping in touch, young fellow, and—" He wrenched himself up to look at Reginald. He was shivering.

The red tide was drifting south, the neon blue receding, and as easily as that, as easily and swiftly as a comet arrives, passes on, and does not return again, not in one's lifetime, the moment for Dias to ask why Reginald had given him the silent treatment, and for Reginald to ask if the letters were never for Alicia out of a well-founded guilt, came and left and would present its chance to be regarded no more. Such nullifying moments exist, and their vacancy is as strong as all else that one might name.

After taking off his coat (he bought a new one every year, to stay in style), wrapping it around the professor, and getting him to his feet, Reginald muttered, "You're ill enough without catching a cold."

Dias slumped against him on their return to the car and slept while Reginald drove, his wet sleeves growing heavier. What answer, even if the question had been asked, could change that Alicia thought so much of Dias? She did not seem to have devised that feeling merely to torment her husband. Dias had possessed her, and she possessed him now, if only in the imagination she tended like an airless bower. Nor could any answer change Reginald's sudden horror for his wife. To carry such an invalid patch of a dream! Dias, even if he had slept with her, maybe even loved her, had never been nor would he be someone for her to go to.

Reginald looked at the sleeping professor. The motion of the car was making Dias's fingers twitch. Dias the collector, the gardener, the man with a suitcase or a book or a drink or a young woman close to hand. If he could not touch it—"it" signifying anything and everything—if it were not firmly rooted in the world of the tactile, he had no use for it. Reginald steered, speeded up. What good were the heavens, then, to Dias? The stars had to be frightening and appalling.

In Dias's sickroom, the roses were strong. All the arrangements were speaking, some in low tones, saddened by the sight of the man who knew how to speak with them being carried in and placed in bed. The calla lilies kept up a glissando chatter beneath the notes of the roses, and the tiger lilies and carnations, with their contrapuntal spices, spoke too. (Who had brought carnations? Red ones weep for broken hearts, but the others say sharp, strict things.) Reginald forced himself to listen, and he could hear them, faintly. It was right that the professor should lie beneath the blanket of a symphony brought by women. The flowers painted on the vanity dolls were shouting, garbling their lines.

"I want a drink," Dias said, as Reginald covered him.

"Wait here."

"You think I'm going someplace else?"

"I could be a while. But I'll come back."

Reginald went on a treasure hunt that took over an hour. He returned and, on the floor near the bed, set a paper bag filled with what he had found. He poured three fingers of whiskey into a glass. Dias took it in both hands and drank slowly. Reginald poured himself some in another glass. The room was warm, though it was cold outside, and he opened a window. A flood of voices from Dias's garden, and from the firs and oaks on the hillside, rushed in. Reginald could smell them and feel their sounds. He could not understand all of them, because he could not speak the language of flowers as well as Dias, though what he could interpret had come from the professor. He gleaned the trilling of some daisies: "I shall contemplate . . ." It was a shame that stars did not speak. They did their part in blending into the music of the spheres, but that was sometimes so lofty as to be unintelligible.

Dias propped himself up, leaning back against the stained pillows and the carved headboard. He held out his empty glass.

Reginald refilled it, and reached into the bag from his treasure hunt and handed Dias some fennel. When the professor saw it, he held it beneath his nose and smiled as he shut his eyes.

"Would you like to hold every decade of your life? Would you like each one to talk with you?" asked Reginald.

"I'd better do it fast," Dias said, inhaling and exhaling hard against the fennel.

"There's time. I'm not going anywhere."

"Go on."

Reginald was not sure how good a translator he would be. "Fennel," he said. "I don't know much Portuguese, even though that's half of what I am. I learned some from you. But I know that Funchal, the capital of Madeira, where you were born, where my parents are from, means *a place where fennel grows*. Fennel says that it deserves compliments, so the Madeirense were right to honor it. Is it reminding you of your first decade? Of your childhood? I can see you wearing one of those burlap hoods, as the other boys did, so that you could carry the firewood on your head down from the hills. I can see you splitting open sugar cane, and eating the scabbard fish. You are nine years old. There were arguments with neighbors over water, always about the water running in the *levadas* that men died to build. You never talked much about your family, or meeting Anita, who would be your wife when you were nineteen."

He left the fennel with the sick man, and handed him an apple. Reginald reminded Dias of something Dias had taught: Apples were designed to offer everyone the invitation to speak with plants, but then Milton had to go and make them into symbols of temptation—in the Bible, no fruit is named in the Garden of Eden—and to this day apples are misunderstood. They were trying to tempt people not into sin but into listening to the earth more closely. The crack they make when they are bitten is like the sound of a key in a lock, and their white meal runs wet with the knowledge of the language of the land, but people do not listen. They think that the apple's noise is about *do this, not that, sin, sin.*

"Take it," said Reginald, "for your years as a teenager." For the years when no one understands you. For when the first temptations of love arrive.

The apple fit perfectly under the professor's curved hand.

Next Reginald spoke of the oak leaf, and let it have its say about freedom. The young adult years of Professor Eduardo Dias, in the fine days of Berkeley: when he could expound as he wished, flirt, and hike on Mount Tamalpais, where from a distance a sleeping woman seems to lie. He was free to drink the California wines that tasted of oak casks, and to have large parties in his house. Unfortunately, Anita, homesick for Madeira, was beginning her reign of sour tolerance. "Which you ignored," said Reginald. "A mistake, sir, if you don't mind me saying. The oak dislikes restrictions and is only too willing to tell you that you are free of a wife, if that is what you want to hear."

Reginald stood and cracked a walnut open under his right foot. He put the broken shell into an ashtray and gave the pieces of walnut to Dias, who took them and closed his eyes again.

"A man's prime years, his thirties. I left them myself, not too long ago," said Reginald. "A man in his thirties should live near walnut trees, because they sing the praises of the intellect. You were writing your famous book on your theories about the music of plants, and you began your travels to deliver papers, appear on television, talk on the radio. You were a star at the university. Your wife would soon leave."

He took a bottle of witch hazel from the bag. It had been easy to find in the drugstore. After saturating a tissue from a box on the night table with some witch hazel, a pungent and bold speech clamored in the room as he dabbed the astringent on the professor's sweaty, jaundiced forehead.

"A man in his forties should seek out witch hazel, because it is about casting spells, and if anyone did that, I believe it was you. It is about being spellbound one's self, and if anyone's midlife was that rich, sir, I am certain yours was.

"I met you. I took every one of your classes. You seemed pleased to find out that we had in common an island on fire in the sea. Sometimes after we had lunch in the faculty club, we walked out through the Sather Gates and down Telegraph Avenue. A large flower stand was near Cody's Books. I remember once we went to check if your second book was on the shelves, and you pointed at the asters and whatever was there and made me stand on the street until I could hear them. It wasn't odd, doing that—not on Telegraph!

"I drank too much beer at your parties. Alicia drank too much—this embarrasses me—cointreau. What a pretentious, saccharine thing to drink. She did it to be tough, and different, because she was so young looking, with her long straight hair parted in the middle. Her breath smelled of deadly oranges. To me it was exotic. It was confusing too, because orange blossoms go crazy with bridal marches, while the full-grown fruit on the tree mutters about thirst. Milton should have put an orange tree in the Garden. Maybe what I have always liked, but especially then, is the rapture of confusion. So I couldn't guess what to imagine that one night at your house, with you and Alicia and me and everyone else drinking, drinking a lot of whatever each of us drank then. I remember when you put your arm around her, the way you did with most of the young women—though now I suppose you've heard you can get into trouble for that sort of thing—and you offered to show her some lilacs you had planted outside. This was my confusion: If they were purple, they were out there singing about love, but if they were white, they were proclaiming innocence. No one else went with the two of you. I watched from a corner. You never turned to look at me, and neither did Alicia. Sometimes you did things so bold that people thought they had to be above board, when very often they were not. I knew this, because sometimes you told me about your affairs. That wasn't very smart of you. I waited twenty-one minutes. (Hops, plain or in beer, scream about what is rude and unfair, right?) You returned, and Alicia's hair was disheveled, but it was usually like that, or nearly. She stopped drinking after we married."

Reginald could feel Dias listening, as the scent of the witch hazel drew its curtain around them both. The apple and oak and walnut were taunting Reginald with a list of possibilities and reasons as to why Alicia would not confess anything definite to him. Could Dias have guessed why Reginald had been angry? Did Dias's silence right now on the subject imply that he was hiding something or that there was nothing to admit? This grand internal debate was wearying. Idiotically wearying. Reginald felt suddenly old, and it made him generous. "Alicia will want to come and see you," he said. "Do you remember her?" Naturally he would; he was brilliant with names.

"Alicia? Oh, Alicia, yes. How is she?"

"Very well. She thinks of you."

Dias smiled, and spoke evenly. "Then tell her to come say good-bye."

"I will," said Reginald. If in fact something had happened, it was possible that both Alicia and Eduardo regretted what they had done to him, thought Reginald, surprised that he had never added this nuance to the list. It was conceivable that Dias and Alicia did not contact each other because they were not going to wound Reginald again. Or it truly was a crush on Alicia's part, and she refused to let Reginald expose it as nothing more than that, effectively sweeping away such an important part of her dreams. In any case the moment for knowing for certain had passed, out on the beach that night, and the moment was meant to go and not be called back as he was doing now, had done for so long, because it had no right to exist as a point on which three lives would be settled.

"I didn't know you in your late forties or fifties. I was—busy," said Reginald. "I don't know what I was." He picked some lint off his shirt and stuck it beneath Dias's fingers. Lint. Wasted years. Years when the professor was drinking seriously, without Anita. Years when he collected things like those garish vanity dolls, and women.

Dias was lying dead center in his sixties. Reginald should have brought him a corncob broken in half to make it a decade of battles, or nettles for cantankerousness. Something with some fight in it.

Ladies and gentlemen, do you believe it is possible to live forever? No? Then pick sweetpeas. I know they sound sentimental and absurd. They look frail as old men, but listen to how they weave into their song of departure tales of lasting pleasure. That is their gift to you.

Dias groaned in a spasm of pain, then caught himself, as if he had been free-falling. The music in the room from the plants was loud. Reginald could hear it more clearly now, as it tried to buffer the professor's fall through space.

Dias gave out a cry.

The vanity dolls were blistering from the heat of the room, leaving ragged dots of color at their feet. The painted flowers wilting off them, and the ones freed from underneath as top flecks chipped away, were shrieking, "He didn't buy us like this for any collection, you dummy! Hey, Reginald! He paints us! He needs us! He hates being old and doesn't know where to put his preening anymore! Ha—*preening!* That's a good word for no-one'll-'ave-me-no-more, don't you think? So he paints us! We're tired of it, I tell you! Just look at us! Tired! We're suffocating under these vests and khakis and fobs and hats and the dresses of women who think he's too old for them! We're so hot with this much clothing, hot! We're shedding! He's vain! Petals! Petals! Ha, ha!"

Don't listen to everything that flowers say. It isn't so frightening, Eduardo, this falling without the sense that your legs will ever again land upright on the earth. May I tell you what I know about space?

The dome above is busy, with its swan, dogs, archer, and Cassiopeia the beauty and Hercules and the twins, and a dipper for water, and maidens and a goat or two. They're already skeletons, to set an example of what awaits us one day.

Bathe your face in the milk splashed across the night; the maidens and the goats use it too. It is not so frightening.

Go beyond that, to where each star is like a sun. That is where the best thoughts of the swans and Hercules go; it is wonderful.

Go past that, toward the cosmic dust.

It will glow.

Reginald folded Eduardo Dias's hands on his chest, and brushed away the lint.

"Thank you," said Dias, eyes closed. "Thank you. This is very nice, Reginald."

Ladies and gentlemen! Eduardo! Are you still afraid of the unknown? Wary of the fall through space? Put your hands on your ribs. Shut your eyes: Sight as we use it must be let go. Feel your skeleton. Magnify the cells of the organs below your ribs.

Enter the core of a cell. Just one; don't worry. Around its nucleus you will find large molecules, more of them than there are stars in the galaxies. Did you know you were carrying the universe?

Slide down one of the coils of DNA. Reminisce! They contain the story of everything you are.

Magnify again. Read the four letters of the alphabet tucked within the coils. They will spell out whatever you need and where you must go.

Into the atoms that look like glowing dust.

Into the innermost electrons. Say that they look like pollen, if you miss the smell of flowers.

Into the electrical attraction of the core of the atom, where there is dancing. As you danced, Eduardo, so often late at night.

Neutrons and protons colliding, far within the atom. Dots eternally whirling around. Under our highest-powered microscopes, we see those dots clustering, and in our lab we color the photographs in an attempt to understand quarks and leptons, and what we have termed their colors and flavors. What to make of the color-carrying gluons? I don't know.

When we in the lab treat the photos of the farthest extents of the cells we carry, those dots of color swaying together, Eduardo—well, they look like great flower gardens.

Reginald pressed his hand over the professor's hands folded on his chest. Eduardo was breathing lightly.

Touch will be the last sense taken. Until then, hold your hand to your heart to enter the awful galaxy. Let someone touch what you touch; it will be that person's turn to put his hands on his own chest some day.

Live as many decades as you can. If you need vanity dolls, look at the dots of color they shed, and call it a photograph of your ultimate magnification.

Teach others how they carry infinity within themselves. Or if you hear this language from someone who esteems you deeply, speak the stellar words with him, and say:

I shall remember you, and how the grasp of what we learned together sings me to my rest. I shall remember this of you, that you went through my years with me.

ISLAND
FEVER

The mob was yelling at Augusto to stop, but without turning
around he dared them to take away his colors. Cowards! he
thought. Stop, stop it, they screamed, their anger hitting his back
in small hot clouds. He was kneeling at the famous seawall in the
yacht harbor of Faial, painting a smiling crayfish that was holding
up a framed picture of Augusto in a serge suit. You own a boat in
your dreams, someone called out, upset that Augusto was claiming a blank space that belonged to the sailors of the world who
anchored at this Azorean island and added a design to the wall as
a charm against being lost at sea. Augusto invited everyone to get
damn well drunk in one of the waterfront bars of Horta, where
their precious foreign captains were busy drinking themselves
into oblivion. No matter where the boats had started, Faial was
the midpoint, always the world declared that his island was midway, and it made Augusto crave endings, completions, some
proof of endings to fling at the world, until he made himself ill . . .
but how could Augusto explain this to cowards? He shouted that
they should tell the sailors that fat Augusto had as much right as
anyone to leave behind a rectangular plot of something for good
luck. But as he finished the last curve on the smile of the crayfish,
he was too weary to do more than lie like a sideways figurehead on
top of the wall over his work and uncork some wine. His wife and
three sons were pushed forward and pleaded for him to come

home. They cut stark but delicate figures, like the figwood sculptures done by the Faialense. *Augusto, Augusto, our only fault is in loving you as you are!* . . . Out of shame he drank quickly, to take everything in in one hard flow . . . but to what end? By his second bottle, the mouths in the crowd, including his wife's, were chattering like bivalve castanets. He could not understand them, and drifted oceanward toward the voices of his lost loves. The bottle slipped from him and shattered near the open cans of blue and green paint, which sat still against the wall. If he had any courage to boast of, he would jump into a swarm of real crayfish, into the real oversalted sea, with its good fleshy parts too far near the bottom—too far, too far . . . He turned his swimming head toward the people departing one by one, including his youngest boy, who threw a stone and missed him. They left him watching a yachtsman from Finland who was painting the scene of Augusto lying on the seawall over his own painting. The yachtsman captured Augusto flat on his back, and beneath that, a crayfish that was smaller than the original and that held an equally scaled-down portrait of Augusto. Augusto laughed. That was funny! It gave him an idea. He would collect himself enough to go lie over this yachtsman's painting and urge the next voyager to reproduce that scene exactly. Then he would lie over the new spot, and so on and on, until many paintings later their portrayals of him on the wall, and his portraits in the hands of the happy crayfish, in the hands of in the hands of in the happy hands of, would be made up of countless reductions. He would be the subject of paintings nestled inside paintings, with different visions of himself—lying smashed, and in his Sunday serge—shrinking as if to the end of the world's longest telescope. The fleet bobbed restlessly up and down, enjoying the joke. But dreams have no edges, the way the soup of the sea is not in a cauldron that can be gripped on two sides and poured. Stalled on the edge of the wall, he could feel how much worse he was than those who were dreamless. Much worse! Much! He grew as mournful as the lost voices. The sun, leaving, was brighter, then colder. He would beg the future sailors to allow him, as the Finnish man was doing, the small comfort, only this, only this, this, of keeping the reductions of him on the inside of the wall, where he would be weathered but not battered.

THE
JOURNEY
OF THE
EYEBALL

It was the dry season, and the pine needles, when they showered down, were golden. José often came to this thicket at the edge of the clearing. Two thick roots streamed from the base of his favorite tree and offered themselves to him, with a soft thatch of needles at the fork. He liked to rest his head there, because this twin flow out of the tree, rigid as muscle, was Ana. He would lower his head onto the sponge sprouting on the muscle and breathe her name: *Ana. Ana.* In answer the hair on the bark would stand. When he reminded himself that the earth constantly moves, he could sense the roots tensing upward to rock him back and forth, speaking happy nonsense. Tuesday and Thursday afternoons— those were all Ana, too. Hours outside those were endurable as long as he imagined that before him soared a T for Tuesday and a T for Thursday, and he would swing like an aerial artist from the ledge of the first T to the ledge of the second. Then, very bravely, he would grip the end of Thursday and flip backward, high and timed just so, to land painlessly at the beginning of Tuesday. He did this well enough to make it seem that no weeks passed and he was growing no older. Sometimes he persuaded her, on one of their Tuesdays or Thursdays, that her husband would not find them if they spent their time together making love near this tree. Naked she left her rose scent here, and it stayed as a pink veil in the air that he stretched over them to stop her from worrying about privacy, or to shield himself when he was alone, lying like this whenever he could. From dwelling for so long in patience, patience had ripened into faith, a faith that he was bound for reward. It was a point of pride that he never suffered nightmares. Some day he would persuade Ana to spend a whole night with him, because this composure of his dreams was rare among men, and it was one decent real gift he could give her.

One day when he returned to lie in the fork of his tree, large tents filled the clearing to block his way. He had forgotten! Today was the annual day of contests, a tradition in the valley; the day had lost its name since no one remembered anymore what was being commemorated. Every year the day simply materialized. José felt a surge of heroism. Ana would be here. On a day that was not one of their days. Cows were being driven in from a far point toward the northeast, where the clearing widened and stretched to the mountains. Near the northwest edge, alongside the thicket with the tree he loved, dishes were being set on the tops of poles, for people to keep constantly spinning. Women were grinding acorns in mortars to make the special acorn cakes for the festival, though why this remained a tradition no one could say.

"A dollar! A dollar! Acorn cakes!" shouted a woman whose hair was going everywhere with static.

"Win me that stuffed bear! Darling!" women were yelling, pointing at the tests of aim and strength.

"Hurry! Hurry!" everyone was calling out.

Clowns with enormous flat red sausages painted over their mouths milled in the crowd, pouring gin into thin paper cups and drinking it and scaring the children.

"Acorn cakes!"

"Who's the strongest? You, sir? You?" the barker at the strong-man tent taunted the men walking past.

Strips of meat on skewers waited in piles next to the grills.

"Hurry!"

José bought an acorn cake and made one of the acorn women laugh by pretending that it was a discus he was going to throw. That cheerful sound—female—was also Ana. He made Ana laugh like no one else. She was always telling him that.

"What's this year's prize?" he asked, biting into the cake.

She was still giggling. "A keg of dynamite, I hope, and maybe the winner will be smart enough to blow this town up."

That was how people talked when they knew they would never leave, and it was more about loving what was theirs than about hate. It was a language that José had learned in the Azores, on the island of Graciosa, before his parents brought him to California, when he heard the people talk with a violent affection about where they were from. But this town had Ana and the thicket and the tree of her and the veil; everything; it had that park whose green lap went right up to Ana's door, which he had never been through but had often faced from the distance, a door in a white façade.

"Whatever it is, it's mine," he told the acorn woman. He raced from one tent to the next, finding out what the events would be, and what he would have to do for each one. He planned to enter everything.

Cows with paper streamers attached with dabs of tar to their hides wandered around, and the udder of one was so swollen from the heat and pungency of the tar that she was spraying milk. People were darting away from her and squealing, but José went to her and said, "There, there," his eyes roaming as he looked for Ana.

The gold-panning competition was already underway. Onlookers cheered as contestants dipped tin cups into a trough of mud set waist high. José attached wings to his ankles and joined them, his fingers tamping frantically through the mud, as he searched for the yellow pellets that everyone would pretend were gold. He cast his eyes where he could, trying to find her, as he collected enough to stitch the equivalent of the gold braid on a sea captain's hat—what his fisherman father had said were called scrambled eggs. That was worth second place, which was good. If he came in second consistently, he would have sufficient overall points to earn the prize, and this idea of victory after winning nothing outright appealed to him.

He moved on to the boat race, on the lake at the western edge of the clearing, and rowed until his hands were raw. Lying flat in the boat at the finish line, he listened for her voice but only heard the announcement that he was half a minute behind the leader. He had used up enough oxygen to be at a slight disadvantage during the *fado* singing match. He let the mournful Portuguese lyrics speak for themselves, and did not resort to supplicating arms, the way some of the contestants did. Who knew if *fados* were originally sung by the widows of the fishermen who did not return, or by the prostitutes of Lisbon? It seemed the appropriate blues singing for a holiday that had no name and a forgotten meaning. José was pleased to come in third, which did not much change his standing.

During the artichoke juggling, the thorns tore his hands. He came in second there also, and he did well in the mile run, the potato-sack race, the weight lifting, and the discus throw. Everyone applauded and laughed when his discus flew off course and struck a clown. José gave the audience an exaggerated bow, his eyes moving around to see if Ana could be found watching how well he was doing. At the lasso competition, he did a complicated dance in and out of the rope that he swirled in a loop.

On the way to the final event, the tower climbing, he leapt into the center of three young women playing catch, grabbed the ball, and pretended to be a seal by balancing it on his nose. He would not give it back until they said "please." He glanced around but there was no Ana laughing at his performance, and the women were annoyed when he somewhat sheepishly tossed them their ball.

By the time he reached the tower, he was tired, and the other men had a head start. But he was tall and that would help him edge some of them out to win the final points that he needed. Ropes hung over walls that were built of scaffolding and hammered together into a high octagon, with small wooden blocks nailed in at intervals as footholds. Twisting a rope around one of his legs, he began climbing hand over hand. At the first foothold, he was surprised at how his arms ached. He had pushed harder than was necessary in the boat race. By the second foothold, his eyes were swimming, and the crowds gawking below were hazy, like something he was attempting to remember. He tried to guess what he might win. The prize might be only a gold cup (pretend gold), but Ana could hide it under a floorboard in her house; she could stand where it radiated upward and feel it travel throughout her. From where he was, he could look past the clearing and plates spinning on poles to the tree in the thicket, and it reminded him that all he had to do was locate the pink veil in the mass of bodies below. He recognized the three women who had been playing catch, now watching solemnly, their necks stretched up like swans'. As his eyes swept again over everyone, he found the rose glimmer with Ana in its center, possessing the gravity she had from her substantial bones—generous gravity. A short, stocky man was resting his hand against the back of her neck, where the tips of her blonde hair lay, always, neatly. She was laughing at something he was saying. Was it the laughing done by married people who did not love each other but wanted to reassure others that any fighting would be done at home, no need to fear an emotional scene? Because it could not, really it could not be the best kind of laughing, the sort that reveled only in the moment, the sort that was José's job. He glanced back at the tree to get his bearings and finish the race, but a spell of vertigo made him shut his eyes, and a pain shot through his side. His side was still splitting as they propped a ladder up to where he was and carried him down.

They had him fastened in the cucking stool before he knew it. A long wooden arm, with the stool at the end, extended over the lake. His feet dangled over the water, and his arms were tied down to the arms of the stool. What was this? Punishment? For what? He heard the roars of laughter as the cucking stool plunged him into the lake with a force that drove water into his nostrils and up behind his eyelids. Dripping sheets of the lake covered his vision as he emerged gasping, "What did I do?"

"Did everything but still didn't win. This is the consolation prize," said one of the lever operators, very matter-of-factly, as if that explained anything. Again they let the arm fall, and Zé's brown hair waved like the plants underwater as he blew his breath out slowly. They kept him without air until his nerves started to spasm, then hoisted him up. He told himself that he could survive even this, that in the old days they constructed cucking stools out of toilet seats to humiliate the victim further, and they had spared him that. When they were through with their fun, they would explain how he could enter every contest and achieve so much, all but the tower climbing, and how none of that counted. How so many second-place finishes did not add up. Down he fell again, into the water.

He rose again and twisted around, because it entered his head, with a fierce brightness, that Ana could prevent this. It was her chance to declare herself, to her husband and in public, by shouting that this absurd spectacle had to end. She would say that it had to stop at once, or else they should let her join him down in the water. He waited, listening, contorted as he looked behind himself. His eye did not catch hers, because her husband was leading her away. But one of her arms was extended out from her side. Had she been pointing and saying, I must go to him?

The crowd hooted at Zé as they sent him down for another ducking. The barrage of options began: She had held out her arms and called for him, and her husband, ashamed, was pulling her away. Or her husband had whispered, "Let's go home to bed," and she was running off with him, and that extended arm was meaningless, only a result of impetus. Or she had held out her arms in the kind of sympathy that any decent person should be professing. Or she . . . he could not think. This was the story of their years together: some motion of her body, followed by him assigning a stream of interpretations to it. His brain grabbed the pictures out of his eyes and bit around their edges and slobbered on them, and the eyes wanted their art gallery, their pictures of Ana, for themselves, without warnings or meaning. As the cucking stool pulled upward, his eyes refused to go back up and see anything more. The brain could not be trusted to leave a sight of her alone, free of its miserable comments. The pressure inside his head expanded and pushed against his eyes. As his body was raised in the chair, the eyes saw a last bid for comfort and hurtled from their sockets. A fish ate one, but the other eye hid among some reeds and waited. It watched José leave the water, his shoes forming little islands on the surface of the water before they disappeared as well. The eye was cheerful. Now it could find Ana and say: The eyes have it! I only have eyes for you! The king and eye! That would have her laughing. He would say, Put me between your breasts, explain nothing, let us go into town together.

The eye trailed enough optic nerve to use as a propeller to reach the surface, swimming through splinters from the cucking stool. José's body, strange to the eye now, stumbled off, behind a dispersing crowd that did not seem to see him.

The eye was free to journey to Ana. Free to do it without the brain! It shivered in a breeze, enjoying how the wildflowers stood as big as exotic trees. Although the eye was nothing but sacs of fluid and membranes, and a photo album holding poses of Ana, it rolled on unafraid, scaring off the insects that got in its path by staring them down. Dragging the rigid nerve sticking out of it was difficult, and the cornea was getting scratched, but Ana could bathe the eye when it reached her house.

The town was more frightening, with the heavy, dirty soles rising and slamming down. The eye felt its humors, aqueous and vitreous, liquefying slightly under the heat of the sun. Making a game out of spinning within the grooves in the sidewalk did not work, and friction was wearing the optic nerve down to a stub. It was exhausting to keep rolling backward and looking upward to guess who was attached to the shoes and socks and stockings. Such a confusion of legs! A high heel struck within an inch of the eyeball. It called out to Ana, to tell her that it was not sure, on this level, how to find her house from here, and its pupil strained, with light entering and leaving through the black hole, but no sounds came out. The eye would have to speak to her by looking deeply at her, when its journey was over. A drop of fluid would glisten on its surface, and in the drop would be shimmering one of the pictures of her—Ana standing by a sea that was like crushed-glass marbles behind her, or Ana standing outside his window once with her blouse undone—and Ana would smile to show that she could see the picture that the eye was holding out to her on its convex screen. Taking the drop that contained the picture on her fingertip, she would put it onto her own eye, like a contact lens.

Another heel! The eye dodged it and got trapped inside a cuff with crumbs and dirt. After feeling its host carry it a block away, up some stairs, and into a smoke-filled room, the eye bounced out of the cuff to peer around. There was Luís, and some other philatelists who were members of the Luso-American societies, the U.P.E.C. or União Portuguesa do Estado da Califórnia, or the I.D.E.S., the Irmandade do Divino Espírito Santo. The eye recalled how José envied the comfort they took in groups, in their projects and festivals. Like them, José was an immigrant, but he felt too singularly like a transplant waiting for the body to belong to, like a living organ sitting on ice before implanting. The eye was getting confused. The philatelists met on Fridays. How could almost a week have passed since the festival? Surely it was still Saturday.

"Luís!" the eye shouted, then reminded itself it could not speak. Ashes on the floor made the eye tear up. A hand dropped down like a falling palm tree and grabbed the eyeball, which soon felt itself being pressed against one of the mint-flavored hinges that are moistened and attached to the back of a stamp to prepare it for an album. At first the mint was pleasant, and going from hand to hand was like spinning in a gallery that was the right size for an eye. Islands, singers, birds, orange antelopes, and foreign powers flashed into view while being readied for mounting. The eye was dazzled. It also caught fractured snapshots of someone's pipe, a broken vein, and the black glasses of a philatelist who pushed the eye so hard against a hinge that it had no more tears left to give.

"Hey, this thing is dried up!" shouted Luís, inspecting it.

"I'm not! I'm not!" said the eyeball. For the barest of flashes, it missed its mind.

"Another useless invention!" said a philatelist.

"Useless!" came the echo.

"Useless!"

The eyeball was thrown out the open window and landed on summer-hard ground, barely missing a piece of glass. The breezes played through the tattered optic nerve, turning it into a wind instrument issuing a high, lone sound, but the eyeball was reasonably blissful. From the sun's height, it figured it to be midafternoon, the time on Tuesdays and Thursdays when Ana came to him. She would kiss the underside pounded into tenderness by the stamps. As the eye pitched forward, the sky tilted, then vanished, then reappeared again, in inverse rhythm to the ground rounding itself into a curve and then going flat. The eye could see the points of the firs or their solid trunks, but not both at once, and after a while it seemed as natural as drinking a glass of water to have the world so divided.

During one of these rotations, the eye failed to spot the foot that kicked it. It flew a long while before landing on a green lawn of fibrous tufts. The kick left the eye's vision blurred, and in the dimness it wondered if it were a boy again in the Azores, seeing the women in their doorways doing their embroidery in the last light of day—God's light—because electricity was too expensive. The rooms glimpsed through the open doorways darkened steadily. To laugh whenever possible—in a vague way, José's resolve to do this began with those women. They worked a lifetime on beauty but never seemed to win a lighted house. He would shout jokes to them, and they would look up for a moment, just one, to laugh with great joy—suddenly a pole lowered and knocked its blunt end against the eyeball, sending it spinning into other hard globes its size, with a shock so intense the eye asked aloud if it had died. And wondered how it could recall something in José's memory, despite the brain and body being gone.

The eyeball had landed in a pool hall. Double vision prevented the eye from focusing on the stomachs leaning over the table. Men were growling and smoking cigarettes. One player was chalking up a cue stick, and a fine dust sifted down. The eye tried to contract its muscles and use the stub that remained of its optic nerve to project itself off the table, but the hand holding the stick lowered to form a bridge, and the eye was struck again. The impact as it hit a mass of balls split open the sclera, and the eye's insides began slowly leaking. It was then that the eye, surprised that it continued living, told itself that maybe not everything could be survived. "My, my," it sang, to cheer itself up. "We got trouble, right here in River City. What rhymes with . . ." but none of the players was laughing. They looked underwater. The eye shifted around to watch the little river leaving it, with the pictures of Ana drifting away; this by way of the eye saying its prayers. It pushed itself into one of the side pockets and rested in a moist pouch, the stitching and padding like a gauze bandage.

It was grabbed from the pouch and set on the table to face a triangle of brightly colored balls. This is how death looks, it marveled, amused; a formation of petrified eyes. From behind came the blow of the stick.

"Scratch!" someone yelled, and the eye sailed over other green plots, past Tiffany lamps with their panes of black-edged flowers, through the hanging smoke, and out an open window to lie on asphalt among some pebbles. Was it groggy, or was that Zé's body hurrying past? "Zézinho!" the eye said, but whoever it was kept on—and was the hair really gray, or had the kiss shots in the pool hall momentarily removed the color from everything? Gray? That was curious. It was late afternoon, but of what day? The eye recalled the tree with its diverging twin roots, and wondered how to return there. What remained of the eyelid, torn and stained like a blind in a bad motel, lowered down, and the eye, before losing consciousness, begged for some end of what it could not say.

A dog awakened it, picking it up cautiously in a mouth that was fragrant like rotting straw. The tongue was velvet, with those bumps that put everything eaten onto a pedestal of sorts before it is consumed. The eye was ready to surrender, but the dog did not chew it. Thrilling, stupendous! Animals do not always prey on weakness! The eye bathed in the saliva, thick but not unwelcome.

The journey was not lengthy, and the eye was released into the dog's water dish. Green fibers from the pool table floated off the backside of the eye. It bobbed around and saw that the dog had entered through the plastic flap attached over a cut-out section of the door. The eye and the dog were in a yellow kitchen the eye did not recognize, but it was homey. Bits of onion skin, coffee grounds, and some coiled hairs skated across the linoleum floor. Give me this! rejoiced the eye. These fallen things meant that life, full and unclean, was in the house, breakfasts and things frying and hands moving across scalps. The eye could not shake its double vision, but here it hardly minded, since that forced every object to wear the register of the dream of itself.

When a woman entered the kitchen, she was herself and also the wish of herself, attached to her as a ghost. She was wearing a robe. "Bad dog," she said, plucking the eye out of the water dish and setting it in a basket of eggs on the counter, near a ceramic crock of metal utensils and wooden spoons with the pale brown halo given to them by double vision. Was she in her robe because it was morning? Was it morning? Or was it afternoon, and had a lover recently left her? She was leaning with her arms stretched out to hold the sill of the kitchen window as she looked through it, regarding who could say what: Was he gone? Was she awaiting him? Dreaming him up? Or had he departed so far in the past that on weekends, when she did not have to put on new eyes and another face to go to work, she slept uncontrollably?

One female gesture, and the old, heinous litany of possibilities and readings crowded in! The eye was furious. Though the brain was somewhere else, it had obviously left its chemicals where they could continue to bring harm. Why couldn't there be such a thing as a plain picture, without the last particle of a person asking, What? What is it? In fact the eye did want an explanation from Ana: *Your arms; that day; what did they mean?* First it had to get out of this stupid basket of eggs.

The woman set an iron frying pan on the heat. She reached into the basket, seized the eyeball, lifted it, and scarcely allowed it a glimmer of horror before cracking it down hard against the hot rim of the pan. His brown iris, his retina, his humor, his back muscle, everything shrieked as agony seared across it. She lifted the eye and brought it down again, aiming to crack it, branding the stripe in. When it did not open and spill, she threw it into the wastebasket. Senseless, the eye managed to tip itself onto a banana peel to cauterize the injury. When the woman had fried an egg, eaten it, set the dishes in the sink, and gone back upstairs, the eye hurled itself against the side of the wastebasket to knock it over. The dog watched indifferently as the eye escaped through the plastic flap on the door. The diagonal stripe cut through the double vision as the eye rested on a bed below an oleander bush;

the injury would cut through everything that the eye saw forever. It would bear this mark, like a darkened doorway where women labored with their fates unchanging. The eye wanted to tell them: I went half around the world, thinking I would earn a huge, lighted house. I work and work, with the dimming light of my dreams. Where at least is the beauty that drives you women blind?

Stars like sparks danced in the periphery. Despite all of this, the last, most basic of animal drives commanded the eye: *Proceed. Select a direction, proceed.*

North. North to Ana, Ana's house. The park, the door in the white wall. Your knight arrives. The deeds arrayed. See. And now? Now?

The park was there, although the plants were cut in half when he saw them. They waved like welcome banners, blue and green and red, a garden of rich silks. Each separate vision had a slash through it. The sky and flowers, as the eye rolled forward, presented themselves in a wild blend, and the eye recalled that this was not far from one style of perception back in the Azores: Life must be seen densely, with its spears of color, shape, sound, meaning; life not lived in delirium is not mysterious enough to be interesting. The delirium was not suffocating, because overhead and in the sea beyond—what vastness! Such an effort to grasp that!

Ahead of the eye reposed the silent house.

The eye squeezed through a grating over the basement and up a pipe, hurtling toward joints that would brace it for the next upward leap, ignoring the centipedes and silverfish, climbing with a blind trust, until it reached patches of her hair. Tangling itself through her hair, the soap caustic, it emerged into Ana's bathtub, where it forgot itself and skid up and down the smooth porcelain, giddy. It rode the sides of the tub until the centrifugal force threw it out onto the tile floor. Where was her dropped hair? The bathroom smelled of disinfectant. Where was her rose perfume?

The carpet in the hallway was plain. The furnishings were large and expensive but simple. Dustless. The eye did not know what it had expected. It had often imagined this house, and carried the pictures of those imaginings, but always with more edges and crevices. With more shades and textures than this. Something that did justice to Ana. Funny Roman statues, wide hats on chairs, tumbles of books and bottles and photos in gold frames.

In the dark bedroom, moonlight pierced through the slats of the Venetian blinds, remodeling the floor with alternating black and white stripes. A form covered with a white sheet lay on the bed: Ana. Was it night? Her hair was spread out against her pillow, and double vision made it appear that she was sleeping under her own full-length soul, but then the eye saw something that turned it to stone. He was here too. He lived here. He walked on the costly drab carpets that he paid for with the same magic wallet that had bought Ana this huge house. Ana's hands were over her chest, and her husband's were over her hands. The eye could not tell how many hours went by as it watched and waited, rocking like a child hugging itself, back and forth. As the night wore on, the eye moved as slightly as it needed for its sear mark to hide within the dark stripes on the floor, and the white of the eye within the stripes of moonlight, shifting to realign itself with the light and the dark and the hour, until it sat in the puddle it had made under itself. *Your arms folded, Ana: Explain.* Explain why I am awake, and you are sleeping peacefully. Incredible that contentment should be more sought after than love. But she had not only contentment and her clean rooms, but love—José's; he made this house complete. He was the part that made it possible for Ana to live with her husband. How the eye hated the brain that would not leave it in peace! The stupid brain of stupid Jose, who gave Ana the happiness she needed to live with her husband. The eye debated how to climb the bedpost and caress its way up her leg, but the journey was much too far.

Lurching backward, the burned slash bleeding as it crossed the stripes of moon, the eye hastened down the hall, through the drain in the tub, down the pipes, and out the basement. José was not accustomed to nightmares. He was nearing the top of the tower and about to win the day, and was merely exhausted from the exertion required for so many events. That had to be it. A touch of delirium. All that mattered now was the title, the prize, and going out to the clearing, to the tree that was Ana with its golden needles.

First the eye needed to rest and let the pictures stored within it settle back into an orderly pile. The world was spinning and tilting. The eye wanted its wandering body back. The hideous immensity of Eyeness, this Eye, Eye, Eye! Always Eye! No wonder it was like ai, ai, ai, a cry of remorse, disbelief!

No rest was allowed. Three potato beetles surrounded the eye and extended their tubes greedily toward it.

"Well, well, well," said one, his pincers widening and shutting with excitement.

"Don't. Bastards," said the eyeball, but they were already on it and took turns sticking their proboscises into the hole of the pupil.

"Unh, unh," groaned one beetle.

"Hurry with your business and be off," pleaded the eye. Its attackers stretched their jaws with delight. The eye pretended it was not itself as they jabbed it, and when the third finished, they called it dung and threw it down a hill.

The eye begged the magic of the tree to rescue it and explain to what end, what on earth were picaresque adventures about nowadays, when one episode was so interchangeable with the next that there was no deepening into subsequence and consequence? A journey of tests mattered only when a reward waited beyond the final line. To be younger, stronger, and more romantic had to add up to some preferred glory; where was the banquet?

An optometrist walking through the park found the eye and took it home. He was white-haired and appeared to live by himself, surrounded by pretty statues. Talking to the eye, calling it one of his own, he placed it on a pad that suggested alcohol. Putting a metal contraption over his own eyes, the doctor picked up a steel instrument, and the eye understood that it was about to be repaired.

"No," it said, without passion. "Don't make me whole again."

"Quiet," said the doctor. "I won't do anything that you won't be able to bear."

The eye was astonished that someone could hear it. Because it was in such a stunned state, the doctor could perform surgery on it, tightening the muscles, applying salve to the burn, stitching the tear, and placing some clear plasma over the bruised cornea.

The eye woke up by itself, with the panorama in focus but colorless. Everything was black and white. The doctor had disappeared, without leaving a note. What was this strange yard, and why—the eye shook itself. No more questions. The landscape was drained, and explanations were more drainage.

The eye was found by the three young girls who had been playing catch. If they were here, then surely the tower, the final match, was straight ahead; he was only tired. Their hair looked gray in the twilight—or were all of them really so much older? What was the year?

More questions! The eye admonished itself again to forget such things as the girls knelt to poke it. "Look what we have here!" said one.

"There're some eyelashes stuck on it," said one, picking it up and pulling its lashes off. She squeezed them onto her own lashes. That made the eye feel like exclamation points on someone else. She laughed as she said, "I'll look terrific tonight when I dance with the men."

The second, with red hair in a rough flame, took out a knife and pared off some of the repaired cornea, saying that she would place it over her own eyes in the hope that she would view everything more insightfully.

The third took the knife and carved the iris out, saying, "This brown will make a good eye shadow. I have to get up early for work, and it'll make me look more awake at my awful job."

"Try it on now!" urged the party girl.

"Good idea," said the one wishing for insights and answers.

"Yes, yes, yes, take me," murmured the eye as the knife claimed everything that remained. The eyeball felt a part of itself being smeared on the girl's eyelids, changing them into the color of the doorways behind the women of José's youth.

What was left of the eye either dissolved in the firmness of their hands or fell to the ground as muscular chaff. The trio walked on, carrying the pieces of José. His destiny, having lost his body, was to live from this moment asunder on the surfaces of women he scarcely knew. The eye, though not wholly itself, clearly saw that it could only go forward divided like this: One part toward the lukewarm comforts of a job, another toward parties and joking to forget the job, and another going after explanations that do not arrive except in the strangest of codes.

STILL
LIFE

Margarida had just crushed an ant charging toward the bowl of lemons on the tablecloth. Her grandmother, Maria de Amparo, stood at the sink with the Galliano bottle, frowning at the gilt tear rolling over the lip because it would stain the label an old ivory

The ant had been wild, scrambling; blots, especially moving ones, bothered her grandmother.

Maria de Amparo sponged away the sugary tear, then washed the yellow sponge and laid it on a paper towel. (Direct moisture would hasten the wearing away of the tile beneath. Never underestimate how much one drop of water can pound away stone.) Another ceremony of cleansing was finished.

Endless, they are, thought Margarida, before censoring herself with the reminder that now, of all times, she should be patient with her Vovó's relentless cleaning.

You won't persuade her to go. You know how stubborn she is, Margarida's mother had warned.

Vovó poured two liqueur glasses of Galliano, gold-bright as melted tender. The sunlight marking up the floor collected into goblins that jumped onto her legs and tore at her stockings until they were a lace of shadow and light. She kept this floor so polished that one morning she slipped and broke her arm and kept the ambulance attendants waiting as she changed into a decent dress for the hospital.

Margarida begged, Come with me. I'll take you. I know how much you wanted to last long enough to see my brother's wedding.

I can't be seen like this, said Vovó sharply. Margarida should know better.

As Vovó sat down, one of the goblins stabbed her in the stomach.

Margarida colored from her cowardice. What she wanted to say was, Please put this off until I no longer disappoint you. Any day now I'm going to sell my paintings. You'll see I'm not crazy. I'll have a sofa at my art show for you in case you get tired. You'll tell me that my great day gave you a reason to live, as you told my brother that the sole thing worth hanging on for was his wedding. Don't give up, now that his day is here. (After my art opening, I'll find someone to marry, too.)

Do you miss the Azores, Vovó? Margarida blurted. Your father's *pastelaria?*

Stories have it that as a young girl you giggled from being up the whole night dancing, you wore bourbon vanilla behind your ears, you folded butter into pastry leaves that cracked and littered everywhere. Beneath your feet, ecru flowers got pressed into stars. What of those flaxen days that you tossed before you like confetti and left unswept? What sternness, what fear of derision, made you equate being a good American with orderliness? Do you miss your volcanic home?

Too late, isn't it, said Vovó's jaundiced face.

They sipped their Galliano. This same bottle, long and flared as a clarinet, was reserved for Margarida's visits—theirs. Private essence of daisy. A yellow brilliant in its aging. Margarida's brother did not drink. Through these last years, Maria de Amparo the party girl surfaced enough when Margarida visited to whisper, Don't tell your parents! This is our corruption, between you and me! Margarida would laugh and promise. The yellow thread of the drink unfurled inside them, and on the loom of their pointed words, they spun a golden cloth.

Come with me, Margarida tried again. You can stretch out in a pew. I know today means—

Do you? Hurry up or you'll be late, said Vovó, already wiping the plastic cover on the tablecloth. Nothing should upset your brother on his day. Titia Clara is coming to watch over me, don't worry.

Let me—began Margarida.

Hurry. *Leave.* Vovó thrust Margarida's coat at her.

Vovó's scarf slipped. Scabs clung like cinders to her hair, despite her twice-daily washings. Margarida took her coat, looked at the cinders, and began to cry, not knowing what to do with her hands. Into this unkempt display Vovó moved briskly, wiping her granddaughter's smearing makeup. At the door, Vovó permitted a hug. The air was sulfurous, a northern Californian fall. Margarida's mouth pressed into a flat line, and she brushed some loose fibers off her sleeve as she headed for the wedding, bothered by her grandmother's rude haste.

During the playing of "The Blue Danube" at the reception, she rested her head against her uncle's navy lapel. They whirled together past cornflowers, and the bride with her ultramarine handbag, borrowed for the day. He whispered that Clara had called. She had arrived at Maria de Amparo's and found her already gone, stretched out on the bed in her sea-colored burial dress. It figures, he said, that she would attend to the final messy business by herself. She really died days ago, but she held back for you to get here from Los Angeles. Made it barely in time. She adored you, you know. Bragged to everyone about you.

Margarida kept dancing but shut her eyes to be alone with her greenness. She swayed like a new blade of grass, with a prayer: Mary of Support & Protection, I did not see how you hoped to spare me the untidiness, the mossiness of death.

I could not hear you proclaiming to me: I shall shield you from the piercing of my love, because yours hurts me so much, like pins that bind me to you fabric to fabric.

FADO

One morning I could not find Lúcia, my stuffed toy pig. I ran crying next door to Dona Xica Adelinha Costa. Xica buried her Saint Anthony and told him he would stay there until he helped us. Then she kissed me and sent me home. That night I saw Lúcia's cloven hoof jabbing out of my bed, and with a shriek I clutched her in a dance. Xica left Saint Anthony in his grave another day to teach him to be faster in finding what was lost.

When the Californian valley heat pressed down on us, Xica would lift my hair, so electric it leapt to greet her approaching palm, and she would blow on the back of my neck. Summers the fuchsia hung swollen like ripe fruit—the dancing-girls' skirts mauve, cherry, scarlet—and Xica taught me how to grasp the long stamen running up into the core and with a single sure yank pull it out with the drop of watery honey still glistening at its tip. My parents urged me to spend time with Dona Xica. We were lucky to be neighbors. I had never known my real grandmothers, and Xica would never have a real grandchild because a car wreck had made her married son an idiot.

Bicho vai,
Bicho vem,
Come o pai,
Come a mãe,
E come a menina também!

> The worm-monster goes,
> The worm-monster comes,
> It eats the father,
> It eats the mother,
> And it eats the baby too!

Mamãe walked her fingers up my leg singing this rhyme, and on the final line she attacked my stomach until I squealed with laughter. I would beg her to do it over and over. *O bicho* never got to my throat. I kept him down where it tickled.

I met worse night-things as I grew up. If I stared too long at those red and white pinpricks in my dark room, they rolled into constellations that burst alive, into pirates and dogs speaking guttural English. When they came for me I would sign crosses in an invisible picket fence around my bed. The beasts roared, but none of them could get me.

One night I finally kicked my sheets over the cross-fence and thought: Climb in with me. Xica is not afraid of you and neither am I. I am more afraid of being alone.

The old stories said that our Azorean homeland was Atlantis, rising broken from the sea. We all have marks and patches surfacing on our skin. I have a fierce dark animal erupting from my side.

Xica had a wine-colored star in the cove at the base of her throat. When she drowsed in the sleeping net that swung between two trees dividing our yards, I liked to touch the star and the bones of her face. She had a long nose ridge, arcing like a dolphin's spine from between her eyes. Inside her hands and chest more bones floated, like those soft needles that poke unmoored in fish's meat.

My fingers could never drink up the rheum that always trickled from beneath her closed eyes. We are so sad, so chemically sad, that it leaks from us. The *fados* wailing from our record players remind us that without love we will die, that the oceans are salty because the Portuguese have shed so many tears on their beaches for those they will never hold again.

Xica Adelinha Costa could faint at will. She would quicken her breath toward that giddy unlatching when the spirit shoots from the body. Then all is cold and black, with a prickle of nausea. One day when I was thirteen I fell with her at the Lodi post office. We were in line to pick up the ribbon *do Nosso Senhor do Bonfim* sent from her cousin in Brazil, and suddenly Xica could not wait anymore. She shook so much I shook too, and then she collapsed into my arms and drove us both to the floor.

Most townspeople already knew that when Xica could not be without something another moment she hurled herself into the dark. Postmaster Riley did not rush over, but he tossed me Xica's package. I unwrapped the thin blue ribbon *do Nosso Senhor* and tied it around her wrist. She woke up because now she could make her pact with God. Xica whispered this prayer:

O Nosso Senhor: Heal my child. He has not spoken a single word since his accident.

O Nosso Senhor: You threw my husband off that whaling boat and did not return him when I was young and pretty in Angra— lift the fog from my son.

O Nosso Senhor: Make his wife love him again.

When the knot broke on its own, those wishes would come true. "Rosa," she said, "I can almost hear my boy saying my name." She smiled at the man offering her water and kissed the wrist tie that marked her as a woman of divine desires.

For sprawling in public with charms, my parents made me recite all the rosary Mysteries—the Joyful, the Sorrowful, and the Glorious—to scrub out my soul.

My father's lavender soap always drew me from sleep. The male-flowering scent came for me before dawn, as he padded around the house until his veins breathed open. He insisted I do his morning exercises with him. Out with the violet bristles protruding from the artichokes, there in the dark-claret light.

"Inhale with me, Rosa," said Papai.

In—let it fill you—*out*.

Sister Angela, my eighth-grade teacher, explained the heart:

Old tired blood of night and sleep starts out purple.

It goes through the heart to wash itself red.

The morning sky is red and purple to remind us that we
    walk in the air of burst hearts.

I would sit on the porch awhile holding my father's hand. It was the first time I already missed someone I still had, and my first lesson that true joy creates not memory but physical particles. My Lodi mornings hid embers in me that will float upward when I die, to burrow in someone else, because they have nothing to do with dust.

Mamãe would bring out mayonnaise-and-tomato sandwiches. We ate together before my father left for his milk route, and then she and I would go back to bed. Sometimes it is beyond endurance, the separateness of all our lives.

Manuel was soft and red-streaked as crabmeat now instead of big-framed and handsome. Xica led him by the hand and said aloud what everything was. He never spoke, but she refused to give up. When her ribbon broke she wanted him to awake with the world already learned. She told him about things that could be held:

Brier roses: Same genus as the strawberry. But you would never guess they were one family. Perfumed, pink. Careful how you touch it, love. Not a few big thorns but a hundred little stabs.

Cat: Venha cá, gatinha, gatinha! Here kitty kitty. It brushed your legs and then disappeared, Manuel. *Até breve, gatinha.* Don't cry, Manny.

Rocks. They stay in one place even if you turn away. Let me brush your fingers against them for you.

Brick: Watch me scrape my frayed ribbon against it to hurry your cure.

Before school I took Manuel's other hand. His wife Marina sat watching. An earthworm sometimes stitched its way around her bare toes in the mud, but she did not move. She liked belly crawlers: A recurring tapeworm let her stay thin and eat madly. We all ate pork—*vinho d'alhos, torrêsmos*—laden with invisible cooked trichinae, but only Marina would not flinch at finding alive in the ground what also churned dead in our stomachs.

In terrible heat she poured honey water or lemonade on herself, whatever was near in the pitcher, and her skin glistened with sugar. Marina was twenty-three, four years younger than Manuel, the most beautiful animal I will ever cross.

Because Manuel said nothing, Xica's morning lessons often veered off into history stories:

Lace: This at my throat, from my sister Teca. She lost her husband off the same boat that killed your father. She went blind hooking lace webs the old way, with an open safety pin. Flowers and faces white and matterless as the drone after the hive sucks him dry. The drone is left jelly. The drone is soft quiver.

Rosa Santos: Her blood grandparents are all buried home in the islands. Rosa came here as a baby and does not remember her birthplace. She has no brothers or sisters—her birth ruptured her mother's tubes.

Because Manuel still said nothing, Xica sometimes cried untranslatable words, things that could not be held or seen, anything that might unfasten the spirits in him:

Marulho: No single English word describes this roar-sound of waves as they crash on shore, Manuel. I think of the *mar* in *marido* filled with *barulho*, noise: an ocean inside a husband crashing. I watched you pace that night and drive off wildly because you could not stand being without her. She was only having coffee with a friend. She wasn't with another man. Marina can't tell time! She doesn't think!

Desacato: The purgatory where someone has not yet said good-bye, is playing along with another person's desires, but not out of love.

Saudade: More than longing. More than yearning. The aching person can declare: *Come to me. Although you are so much in me that I carry you around, I'll waste away if fate keeps us apart.*

Marina: You crashed into a tree and lost your mind over her. Stop fussing, Manuel. Rosa and I will lead you to her. The lazy goat Marina.

At the sound of her name his hand opened.

The Portuguese families in Lodi kept canaries. Some also raised parakeets or talking mynas and parrots. The birds gouged their cuttlefish and filled our houses with trilling and cracked seed. We needed their song to match our pulse and high nerves.

Mamãe wanted to murder the plumber. Mr. Fernandes fiddled with the leaking pipe under our sink until it lay quiet. Mamãe paid him. The next morning she needed him again. Mr. Fernandes returned three times. Finally the drips turned the under-sink cabinet into moss, and one night the pipe blew up. After shutting off the main, my silent mother drove our soaked towels to the plumber's house. She nailed them over some windows so that Fernandes would look right into mildew.

When she returned home she sang an aria with our birds.

Two lines from a *fado* my father often played:

> *Navegar é preciso,*
> *Viver não é preciso.*

This song of fate has two translations:

> To navigate is precise,
> To live is not precise.

or:

To navigate is necessary,
To live is not necessary.

A widow in our parish wrote a *fado:*

As a child I thought love was for angels,
But fate says that love is the unbroken horse
Dragging us behind its sleek smooth haunches
From the moment we taste it
To the day we die.

Manuel had once loved to comb the great matted snakes out of Marina's long hair. Every day in the sunlit yard he untangled her black knots, fixed a braid, and tucked flowers into her hair. She would lean her head back to kiss him with her upside-down face. They laughed when the kissing ruined the braid and Manuel had to do it over again.

Xica would bring out a pitcher of water flavored with cut peaches. She knew the most ageless secrets, my Xiquinha: The peach wedges looked like prawns with fibrous legs dangling, the scarlet legs that had clung to the peachstone's rutted face. She could take plain water and change it into an aquarium.

Xica left me when I still had so much to ask. When she set down the peach water for the lovers quietly, barely looking at them so that nothing would crack the spell, I should have asked the color and shape of the physical particle this love engendered. Maybe it is that blue anchor in the seat of all flames.

During the Lodi heat we called knife-fight weather, Xica decided that Manuel wanted to relearn his wife's hair. We led him to her and used his clay fingers to tug her hair into rough skeins. Finally one morning the pulling made her wrench away and jump to her feet. "Stop it!" she screamed. "It's hurting me! It hurts!" She pushed us aside and ran off.

Manuel's half-closed eyes fluttered. "Marina," he said: his first full word since the accident.

Xica and I grabbed him. "Say it again," we pleaded. "Marina. Say 'Marina.' Say anything."

He could say nothing else and turned to watch her recede in the distance.

Marina's flight became the first entry in Xica's *Ofensa* ledger. Inscribing sins and proposed punishments in a great book was God's job, but once again He was asleep. Xica opened a large black diary and wrote:

#1. Marina Guimarães Costa, December 10. She abandoned us. Sawdust in her food will slow her. I'll turn her into a tree.

When boys started coming to visit me, I saw almost nothing of Xica and her wars. I set the table for my callers and bit my lips hard to make them red and swollen. Milk cartons then had lovely thick wax, and boys would scratch out my name with their finger nails. Tilting the cartons to the light I would read: *Rosa Santos loves Cliff. Rosa + Jimmy.*

My father told me to sweat my nerves back inside my skin. One day I had to plant scarecrows through our entire field using tin-can lids. The discs had sharp fluted edges, and I cut myself hammering nail-holes into them. I dragged a full trashbag of them through the tomatoes and fava beans and corn. I tied the lids with twine to stakes. The weakest breeze would lift them, teeth glinting, at the crows. No one in Lodi used straw men anymore. We got our scarecrows from cans.

I stopped planting my buzz saws because inside the thicket bordering our land I saw Marina, her clothes tossed onto brambles, colt legs splayed, with a man I did not recognize pressed to her back. She was in a sweat and did not see me. With a terrible moan the man dug into Marina so hard he lifted her into the air.

I ran home, and the cut metal I had seeded stirred after me.

Marina played with the saucers of glitter and straight pins. The crushed ice was to make the crackled lace candles, but she kept slipping pinches down her dress. She stuck holly into Manuel's hair and splashed the paraffin so that hard cysts cooled on our worktable. I was stenciling angels and wondering why I had come. Ever since Manny stopped working at the dairy, Xica and Marina had earned money doing needlework and raising chickens, and at Christmastime they sold candles. This was the first year I did not want to help. Manny was so peaceful cutting foil stars that I wanted to slap him. Xica was bossy, and Marina was all mouth. She stood at the refrigerator finishing a whole jar of olives, and then she drank the black-salt juice. She always needed to drain everything to its bedrock and bone.

Xica went into a rage when she saw Marina eating everything in sight. She hurled paraffin blocks, snowflakes, and sequined bells so hard toward the kitchen that I knew she had guessed the truth. When Marina escaped through a window, Manuel held out his arms and tried to go after her. We had to restrain him, and he fell down into the Christmas debris and twitched with shock. Xica and I rolled him onto a huge, padded tablecloth. We hoisted the ends and rocked him like a child in a hammock to stop his crying. Manuel spoke the last words he would ever say after his accident: *Marina. Marina.*

"Be quiet, sweetheart. She's here," Xica whispered, nodding toward me.

"I'm here," I said.

I doubt we fooled him, but he quieted down. Our arms soon tired and he sagged to the ground, but we kept swaying, ignoring the tearing of our net, until the waves of lulling finally took him. When Manuel was asleep we got on our hands and knees, graying Xica and I, to pick up the trimmings and the stars.

Some entries I read in the *Ofensa* book of Dona Xica Adelinha Costa:

—*#15. Mr. Alfred Kearny, Lodi florist, January 20.* Fainting not enough anymore. Knocked over ten wreaths when I fell. Still he would not admit he is after my son's wife. Tomorrow I'll pour honey inside his store, and by nightfall black ants will be eating his flowers.

—#*32. Marina Guimarães Costa, March 2.* Twice, three times a day I wash her sheets! She comes home with that sin smell. It will travel down the hall to Manuel's room if I do not scrub and bleach it from her cloth. My hands are turning ghost white.

—#*48. O Nosso Senhor, April 17.* Why did You make her the one thing he has not forgotten? Untie this ribbon!

—#*54. Mrs. Lamont, May 1.* Spreading gossip. To teach her silence I'll phone her five times today and say nothing when she answers.

—#*56. The Sun, May 5.* Too hot. Bug and spider nests in house. Feel poisoned. Hate the Sun.

Xica finally packed Marina's bags and threw her out. Mr Kearny hid her in his guesthouse and told his ragdoll wife it was the only charitable thing to do.

Father Ribeiro took Xica and Manuel sailing at Lake Tahoe. He meant well. Water calls to us if we avoid it too long, and he thought the Costas needed to answer the water's cry. Water would melt Xica's bile and teach her forgiveness, and it would soothe Manuel's heartbreak. I did not want to go, but Father Ribeiro insisted that I was one of the few friends Xica had left in the entire parish.

We were not far from shore. A young woman ran from the lapping water up the sand, tossing her hair as a man chased her. Even on our boat we could see the sparkling curves of their backs. She squealed while leading him farther from us. When he caught her, they collapsed together into a single tumbling dot on the horizon.

Manuel stared after them and suddenly threw off his life jacket. Father Ribeiro grabbed for him, but he was already over the edge.

Xica Adelinha Costa had tried to escape Portuguese fate by moving halfway across the world, to a dry inland patch, but there she was for the second time in her life on a shoreline wailing over the body of a dead man. Father Ribeiro, dripping and gasping, still giving the corpse the kiss of life, could not console Xica.

She grabbed a knife from a nearby picnic table and with one upward slice cut open the useless ribbon on her wrist. The ground was already claiming Manuel. Sand, leaves, and gravel coated his wet skin and filled his eyes and ears. Xica held him and tried to brush the debris away with the lament that convulses newborns, body blind and purple, the lament that told me she had already fallen into another world.

She wanted air to kill her instead of water. The day after she buried her son, she dressed in a long brocade gown and lay in the sleeping net. My parents fed her broth and told her to stop talking nonsense. "I'll be gone before dinnertime," she said simply. She closed her eyes and put her will to work.

Father Ribeiro came by to remind her that Manuel had not actually killed himself—he was a child, and when a child sees what he wants, a flash that speaks to memory, he flings himself toward it. His innocence meant he was in heaven. "So you shouldn't give up heart," Father said.

She did give up heart: She gave it to me. God still owed her a wish, and I was the only one who believed she could hold Him to it. My parents and Father Ribeiro were off discussing which doctors to call when Xica opened her eyes long enough to put my hand on her chest. "Rosa," she said. "My Rosa."

Her heart fluttered like a trapped hummingbird. Perhaps she was drawing all her blood toward it, because it beat harder and faster while her calves drained and her hands, face, and neck paled to chalk. Even the star in the cove of her throat dimmed. She was pulling up a winding sheet inside herself.

"Xiquinha," I said. I felt the bird fly up against her ribs, trying to break through and splatter on my palm. She was straining her heart upward as far as she could, loud and furious, directly into my hand. As I bent my face closer to hear the wing beat, the raging bird exploded, and then my Xica was gone.

After Marina had a miscarriage, Kearny's wife nursed her briefly and then ordered her out of their lives. Suddenly Marina had no more lover and no more baby. She took over Xica's empty house. Soon after Marina returned, I put a conch shell on her porch. No one can resist sealing the cold pink lip against an ear to hear the water echoing. I knew one widow who carried a conch in her purse to clap to her head like a transistor radio whenever she wanted to induce a good sobbing. Marina was such a glutton I knew she would fill herself with tides. She would probably take the shell to bed.

At the drugstore a week later I bought wax-candy skeletons. Children bite off the skulls, drink the cherry-water inside, and chew the wax until it disappears. I set the skeletons in toy plastic boats around Marina's windows and doors. Before leaving for school that day I heard her bellowing.

I punctured every inch of her garden hose. It spouted water everywhere like a gunned whale.

I hesitated after they found Marina aimlessly wandering the highway. Then I heard two women gossiping: *She killed her husband, and now she's queen of the house.* The next day I uprooted some plants from my father's aquarium, slapped them on an old doll, and left it strangling on Marina's porch.

One morning when Marina left to sell some chickens, I took the key from behind her mailbox, entered the house, and uncaged her birds. She would return to find them shrieking and pecking the apples on the table. She would never catch them. I hid hard-boiled eggs and left a typewritten note: *Ten Easter eggs in here. Tear the place up before they rot.*

Certain delicacies in our cupboards were meant to last for-ever—the sulfured apricots, the grosgrain-tied bags of sugared almonds, the port with ashy mold around the cork. I stole them for Michael Paganelli, the boy who had come to work on the Bettencourt ranch. I had just started high school, and after classes he would be waiting for me in his pickup. We ate sweets and drank until I was gut-sick and brave enough to taste Michael's salt by licking his neck. I spanned parts of him: From his left nipple to his sternum was one strained hand stretch. My forefinger and thumb measured him nosetip to chin.

Alone at night I could put him back together. I spread my hand out on my chest and thought: Michael's breastbone is now crushed here. I have captured the size of him. The night breeze lifted my bedclothes as I touched Michael's lengths all over me.

It was worth lying to my parents. It was worth the stealing. My battle with Marina, and even the faces of my beloved dead neighbors, evaporated under the sheer height and weight of my new love.

Sex happens the way a pearl is formed. It begins with a grain or parasitic worm that itches in the soft lining until the entire animal buckles around it. With enough slathering it will relax into a gem.

The first time I made love was in water. Michael and I dove into the swimming hole outside town. The moon came down to be in the water with us, and in its round ghost center I measured Michael's erection so I would have it again when I was alone: more than my hand's widest stretch. Touch anemones at low tide and watch their tissue shudder and their color deepen. When Michael disappeared in me I cried his name, because this was how I had always thought of love—a jolt of swallowing someone alive. Sometimes we thrashed into deeper water. We submerged below the moon and kicked hard to come up choking on it.

Love had odd unforeseen glories. I came not from what he was doing but from arching against his rough belly. I would never have guessed that his tongue in my ear could cause rapture, or that not knowing how to ask him to speak my name could trigger such sadness. The sheer force of his coming thrust me from the water, and suspended in the chill, with stabbing pains and my blood on his thigh, I wondered why people are fated to have this torment forever.

They said the stench of rotting eggs drove her crazy. The house was a shambles, and here and there a myna chipped at the bright eggs putrefying on the floor. Mrs. Riley came by one day with an embroidery job and found the wild-haired Marina in a place smelling like a dead animal.

She took Marina to the hospital, where nurses closed her bulging eyes with cool witch hazel. They spoon-fed her purées and kept a night-light by her bed. Mrs. Riley called half of Lodi with daily reports. After a week doctors said that Marina was not sick enough to keep in the hospital, but she would never fully recover as long as she remained alone.

Michael acted as if he didn't know me. He stopped coming by after school, and when I went to the Bettencourt ranch he looked straight through me.

The next day I returned to the ranch and beat Michael's truck with a plank to chip off half the paint. Rust would set in before he could hammer out all the dents.

When love no longer recognizes us, we fall into the strangest outbursts and comas. I had restless sex with the first boy who came along at school, and then I collapsed into shock. I lay in my room until Mamãe tried to rub my shoulders and ask me what hurt. "Leave me alone," I snapped, wrenching away. That is the final curse of dryness: We forget about those closest to us and dwell suspended upon what has been snatched away. We who are robbed should be forgiven everything.

We recaged the birds, and I taught the mynas to speak so that the empty house would ring occasionally with throaty words. Marina liked the snapdragons and lilacs I planted for her. Marina: Do you recognize that plant there? It is what we call Our Lady's grass. Dozens of Azoreans smuggled it over here because they could not survive without its penetrating oil, only to discover that it grows wild in the hills.

I know what my punishment will be. Someday I will have to live a long time alone, long enough to imagine several times that I will never recover. Anytime I think *this cannot continue,* my sentence will double. This solitude will come after a great love has died, for then I will not be free so much as haunted with dead perfume.

One day, when mosquito bites covered Marina, I thought of Xica washing bruised Manuel outside in a large metal tub. She would keep the warm water and the soap out of his half-blind eyes, and as she worked, pouring long streams over him, she had such radiance that I knew she had the whole world there in her arms. There was not a trace of anguish as she smiled down at him. When she was done, she would lift the wounded man up into the light. Xica was so splendid before bitterness choked her, so glorious when she bore him aloft.

I found Marina writhing from bug attacks. They loved her sweet blood. I mixed some baking soda with water, and while cradling her I dabbed it over her itching red sores. I would have to keep the worms and spiders from chewing her. Marina could not stop scratching, and I remembered a touch my mother would give me when I was afraid at night. She would run her thumbs up under my eyebrows, along the bone and out to the temple. This sweeping over my eyelids always melted my nerves.

Marina rested back against my chest while I put her to sleep with my mother's eye-stroking. Here is the seal from which all grace comes: We must create Pietàs in order to live. Flesh that is torn, flesh that is dead or dying, even as it is rotting through your fingers—hold it next to your heart. Find ripe and tender flesh too, and hold it in your arms, because your life depends on it. Hold it for as long as you can, and ask for its blessing.

THE REMAINS OF PRINCESS KAIULANI'S GARDEN

"My stomach is singing!" said King Kalakaua.

The children lined up along the wooden wall sensed their stomachs singing also—they always did, when Frank Vasconcellos played his musical instruments, especially his *braguinha*—but they were afraid to move. For one thing, their mothers had warned them that not so long ago, if the shadow of a commoner fell across the path of a king, the offender would be killed. Times were changing in Hawaii, but it was still a good idea not to make Kalakaua wrathful. Elena, Frank Vasconcellos's daughter, tried to catch the eye of her mother, Amelia, but she was sitting up very straight. A royal retinue was in their house, visitors were in attendance, and she could not allow herself to uncoil toward the music. It was a shame. Her mother wanted so absolutely to do the right things that would allow her to belong to Hawaii before she died, without stopping to think that such a rigidness ensured that she never would. Pinned to Amelia's dress was a camellia as white as her hair, and it did not flutter to the music; she would not allow it.

Elena did not think the king looked prone to wrath. He was wearing gold medals on a white suit that people said he had bought in London on a triumphal sweep across the world. They said that the cloth had been woven by naked women who had shaved their heads and bodies so as not to get a single stray hair on the material. Kalakaua looked like a messenger from the sun. Everyone was both afraid to look away from the king and afraid to look directly at him. Just the way they behaved toward the sun out in the sugarcane fields. Only her father, filling the room with the high sweet sounds that made it possible to think of motion in this heat, was in his work pants, the denims that someone far away in San Francisco had invented for the gold miners. Friends thought he was arrogant to wear something associated with gold. Even Elena's mother thought so.

The king had heard about the marvelous new instrument that the Portuguese had brought to his country and wanted to hear it for himself. He was tired of the instruments made of gourds and pebbles. Frank had completed his sugar contract the previous year and decided he wanted to make more than ten dollars a month, and was now one of Oahu's best *braguinha* makers and players. He also made the *rajão,* the fiddle that the workers in the taro patches liked. After arrangements were made for a concert, Kalakaua and his attendants had arrived in a lacquered carriage at the house of Frank, Amelia, and Elena Vasconcellos on the slopes of the Punchbowl.

A sharp point stabbed the back of her neck. She had ironed her dress so well that the loose threads were sticking her. Her high-buttoned shoes were pinching, and she was sorry that she had brought them all the way from the Azores. She had had three months on the *Priscilla* to fling them overboard. They were use-less in Hawaii. Besides, it took a long time to button them, be-cause her hands were too large for the rest of her. They were the result, everyone said, of having parents who married old. It was as if her mother and father had had many large dreams at their wedding but not enough strength to do more than give them to a single part of their offspring. Elena's hands hung down like huge pincers attached to a tiny lobster. In a strange way, she missed the old days when she had to fight all the time, her hands in enor-mous hard fists, to stop her friends from laughing at her. Now they ignored her because she and her parents were not coming back to sugar.

> . . . _Giroflé, giroflá,_
> _Giroflé, giroflá!_
> _Flé, flé, flé!_
> _Flá, flá, flá! . . ._

Frank was singing nonsense as his fingers plucked the _bra-guinha_. The king loved the music with its meaningless words. He leapt to his feet and danced around the room, a strange cross between a waltz and something like a hula. Elena caught her mother looking aside, embarrassed. It was rumored that the king had had over one hundred hulas composed at his birth in honor of his penis. Elena had overheard some old women gossiping about it one day, and they scolded her for listening in. But how was having ears her fault?

Her father's music filled Elena with such wonderful sorrow.

"Flay, flay, flay!" shouted Kalakaua.

Frank, too, was jumping around the room, with the instrument cradled in his arms.

The listeners tensed. Kalakaua kept coming close to crashing into the buffet table lit with kukui nut-oil lamps, and covered with an offering of sweets, doves made of pulled sugar, tarts, pumpkin jellies, banana pies, the orange-flavored strips of fried dough called _coscarões_, candied papaya, and flans. Elena thought her mother was going to collapse. She had gotten up at midnight to begin the final round of baking, saying that since the hour hurt, the food would taste better. Elena dug her fingernails into her palms, the size of grapefruits, to stop from giggling. She looked over at her best friend, Madelena, whom she had met on the _Priscilla_ when it was dawning on them that they were leaving the Azores forever. Madelena smiled back. Elena hoped this meant they would visit later. Sometimes she was not sure about Madelena. Ever since her father had decided that the Portuguese should follow the example of the Asians who were pushing their children out of the fields toward the trade life in Honolulu, Madelena had not been coming around as much. No one had, until the arrival of the king today.

"_Auwe!_ Bloody hell!" he shouted. He bumped into the table, and two of the attendants carrying the huge feather standards, the *kahilis,* rushed over to grab the dishes falling off the edge. They caught them without dipping the *kahilis.* Elena was the only one to applaud their skill. Kalakaua turned to grin at her. Frank kept playing. She felt everyone staring, and after holding her head up and smiling a moment, then seeing that Madelena was frowning and so was Amelia, she looked at the floor, and at her uncomfortable shoes, and at her hands that were too awkward to fold neatly in her lap.

Her stomach would not sing again until later, when everyone was huddling near one end of the buffet table, holding a treat on a crisply ironed serviette but feeling too nervous to eat anything, and she abandoned her friends to walk over to Kalakaua. His presence was so immense that she was not afraid of him; her hands had taught her how to be fearless about dimensions in flesh. He was descended from the Polynesian gods and wanted to be the emperor of what the natives were beginning to call Oceania. He was eating a coconut tart. A strand was trapped in his black beard. Her stomach began a mild melody that picked up in tempo as the king took the tissue paper from beneath the tart, its edges cut in a fringe by Amelia at dawn that morning, and held it out toward the attendant.

"You look like my little niece, Kaiulani," said Kalakaua.

The attendant, reading the king's mind, pinned the square of fringed tissue paper onto Elena's dress, so that it looked like a funny paper medal.

I'm not Portuguese, she thought, not any more. I'm Hawaiian.

She reached over to the buffet table and pulled a square out from under another one of the tarts. It looked very small in the center of her palm. An attendant took it from her and hesitated. Kalakaua nodded, and the attendant pinned it onto him, next to his gold medals. Elena and the king laughed, and her stomach sang, "Enjoy your moment with the king! You have lost Madelena!"

It was true. Not long after the party, Kalakaua ordered three dozen *braguinhas* from Frank, asking him to bring them to the Iolani Palace.

When he returned home, he threw his moldy cap in the air. "I'm rich! I'm rich!" he shouted.

Amelia looked up from her darning. "What does that make me?"

"The wife of a rich man!" Frank shouted. "What you've always wanted! You may applaud!"

Elena disliked how her mother bit threads off with her teeth. Everything, it seemed, connected to her claim that it was all well and good for her husband to be able to race about, forgetting to act his age; she had been pregnant at age forty-three, when her husband had been forty-nine, and now she was physically a mess, it was too much to stand and walk the ten paces to get the scissors when she did the mending. Better to use her teeth, before she no longer owned them.

Elena sometimes cringed in her clothes, from imagining her mother's spittle dried into the cloth. That was why she ironed everything so firmly.

"They loved me!" said her father, taking gold coins out of his pocket.

Elena put two of the coins over her eyes, to feel how round and cold they were, until her mother snatched them off and said that was a bad omen; that was how the dead had their eyes closed.

Often after that the king requested that Frank come play at royal parties, and because he was small and vigorous, the Hawaiians called him the Jumping Flea, or *ukulele*. It then turned into the name of the *braguinha*.

"Well, if it isn't the princess!" Madelena yelled one morning at Elena.

The tissue medal was starting to melt off Elena's dress. She had hoped to wear it every day for the rest of her life.

"Princess! Princess!" shouted some of the old women, when they passed her on the slopes of the Punchbowl that led to the road into town.

"Princess? Not with those hands! She should be a hand-maiden!"

Elena could not fight old women. Like her mother, they were too mysterious. A certain class of them—not many, but enough to constitute a minor phenomenon—possessed a knowledge that made them quite starched: They were the ones who had married when young and suddenly, without explanation, returned to their childhood homes during the week after their wedding, to live alone past the deaths of their parents and into old age. It was understood that this was not to be commented upon. Two of these women lived here on the hillsides, and though Elena had left the Azores when she was nine, she remembered a few of them there, too. What a shame, to have elegant weddings, and then to pretend that the whole event had never occurred. Elena truly did not understand people. Why couldn't anyone say what had happened to these women? Why couldn't they be friendly to a king? What good did it do to be lunas, standing in the field ordering other people around and ending up being hated as much as if they had quit the fields entirely?

"Princess!"

"No! The handmaiden!"

"She looks like little Kaiulani, the little niece!"

The taunts, and the boys saying endless crude things, made Elena's hands swell up, until they were half again as big.

When Frank had first started making *braguinhas,* Elena and Amelia did the cooking and running of errands, to give him the time he needed. But now, with people from the court and elsewhere wanting ukuleles, new work needed to be done. Elena liked the idea of her family being ukulele people. She would be content never again to go out under the sun where any other human beings were.

She discovered, to her shock, that her hands were incapable of plucking the strings. She had no talent for it. When she begged her father to make her an apprentice, she found that she had no skill with building ukuleles either. He and her mother said it was not something for a girl to bother about, anyway. But it did bother her. She lacked the thing inside, whatever it was, that gave life to music, and she could not teach herself how to fit the frets and strings together. What was she to do with herself? Boys only noticed her to ridicule her hands. She had a long nose and small eyes. She was too short and had no breasts to speak of, even though she was fifteen. The theory that her father's earning some money might make her more attractive did not appear to be working; those hideous hands stayed in the way. And Frank was spending his new income on Honolulu's society parties as fast as he made it.

On one of the rare nights he was home for dinner, he asked Elena, "What're you good at?" They were eating poi and grilled pork.

"She doesn't need to be good at anything," said Amelia.

"Let me hear that from her," said Frank, drinking his champagne. Sometimes he let Elena pour a tablespoon into her glass of water. Amelia was starting to listen to the missionaries and thought champagne was the worst kind of devilry, being light-colored and pretty. She was mad that money was being spent on things that did not last. Elena knew that her father let her drink his champagne because he loved her, but he was too old to do more than look forward to an unrigorous ending to his own life. That included situating these women in his house somewhere amenable to them, leaving him to float away on the strains of the string music that had completed his reasons for being.

"Excuse me, your highness," said Amelia.

Frank laughed. His refusal to jump into a fight with her was going to exasperate his wife into an early grave.

"I don't know," said Elena. The poi was what the Hawaiians called two-finger, because its thickness required that many fingers to scoop it up. She watched it solidifying.

"Think," he said. "Everyone I talk to about marrying you off says you have crazy ideas."

"It's you. You're the one with the crazy ideas," said Amelia, not looking at her daughter. "Elena is neat and clean. Boys nowadays have these absurd glamorous ideas. She does the best with what she has."

"They're those hands she's got on her."

"Shh."

It seemed to Elena that her mother was quieting him more from her own wretchedness about having a daughter with bloated hands, and not because Elena might be upset.

"Everyone is good at something. Can she bake? What's she good at?" said Frank.

Elena was accustomed to them speaking as if she were invisible, and did not blush. They were only saying what everyone knew. "Why are you asking me this? I can dance," she said.

They turned to look at her.

"No daughter of mine is going to learn the dances they do around here. They won't let you, anyhow," said Frank.

"Amen," said Amelia.

"Think again," said Frank.

"Well," said Elena, sensing that she had to answer quickly, but that her reply would haunt her. It was a shame that some gift out of the ukulele would not fit into her grasp. "Well, I like to iron. Yes. I'm good at ironing."

"Ironing is a very fine thing for a girl to know," said Amelia, clearing the plates as a signal that Frank should not open another bottle.

Even Amelia agreed that opening a laundry on Beef Street was a fair venture. It was not far from the dry goods store owned by Archibald Cleghorn, the father of Princess Kaiulani, who was in line for the throne. It was also a means of channeling some of the ukulele money before Frank spent it. Elena forgot about her vow never to yearn for places where there were other people. She often lingered on the sidewalk, hoping to glimpse Cleghorn, who had built the Ainahau estate with three lily ponds for his daughter, the future queen. Eight kinds of mango trees, and teak, cinnamon, and soap trees were on the grounds, where peacocks wandered and shook their heads with their antherlike crowns when twelve-year-old Kaiulani called to them. Fourteen varieties of hibiscus and a huge banyan grew on Ainahau. But Mr. Cleghorn did not show up at his dry goods place, any more than Elena's father came by the laundry. It was what he had built for his wife and daughter, and he was elsewhere with his ukulele.

Not far off from the laundry was the ocean, the color of limes. Elena had no time to go there, and was content to come off the hillside in the morning, alongside her mother, and head into the flat part of town, where the carriages went by with a clattering that set off the other music stored tightly in her head. Her mother never said much to her. Her mother would be sixty in two years, and she walked and talked slowly, as if expecting Elena to use her hands to lift off the burden weighing on her shoulders. When Elena did try to talk to her, it was plain that nothing delighted Amelia. To be in Hawaii, to have traveled to a new life, to have work in town, and yet to be so sour!

Elena was determined to be everything her mother was not. Washing clothing invigorated Elena; she got to hide her hands in the tanks of water when she chatted with customers. She had no trouble lifting the heavy baskets, and hardly needed the scrub brushes of torn coconut leaves that hung near the tanks. Her fingers knew how to manipulate the material. She tried to move the clothes through the water in a rhythm that suggested the sounds of a stream, in case Archibald Cleghorn, or his wife Likelike, or his daughter Kaiulani might be strolling past. But despite being the daughter of Ukulele, she could not force the water into a rhythm.

"Stop splashing," her mother would say.

"I'm not."

"Have you finished the order for the Andersons?"

"I just have to tie up the package, Mama."

"Then do it. You don't have time to splash." She would open the spigots on the wall that directed steam onto white sheets.

Elena would move her hands through the water a beat more. "Is Daddy having dinner with us tonight?"

"How should I know? When you finish with the package, here's a dress to iron." Her mother would throw something at her.

One thing Elena adored, utterly, was ironing, which she did very seriously, using the tip of the iron to trace every embroidered edge or seam, following the curve of every stitched border. The size of her hands made it easy to hold the iron upright, a metal ballerina on point. Not even her mother ironed as thoughtfully. Elena went so far as to iron the internal patterns in lace and the monograms on handkerchiefs, almost thread by thread, and she tended to the inner seams of jackets, if they could be reached by lifting the lining. She could not say what was so compelling about ironing. It was a metallic strength that made something clean and new. It was soothing, how easily power or hidden beauty could be stamped somewhere, into cloth, into a person.

That was the reason she loved the story her father once told her about Likelike, Kaiulani's mother, who hid flowers inside her piled-up hair so that everyone would think the scent was issuing directly from her. Elena tried to arrange a gardenia in her own hair in the Likelike style, but her knuckles kept knocking into each other. She came out of the storeroom, where she had been attempting to fix her hair according to her reflection made by a sheet of metal, and asked her mother for help.

"You want me to what?" her mother said, suds from the brown soap coating her arms. She pushed up her glasses and left suds on her cheek.

Elena squirmed. "You heard me."

"We have sixteen orders to finish, and you want me to play with your hair?"

"The orders will still be here. In the time we're taking to talk about it, we could have finished, Mama. I have the gardenia. We can tear it in half, and you can have part of it."

Her mother leaned over the wash tank and roared with laughter. "Where do you get your ideas? A gardenia in your hair! Ooo, you *are* a princess."

"I guess I get my good ideas from Daddy. I sure don't get them from you."

Elena did not back away as her mother came over and slapped her. The stinging on her face remained as she picked up a washboard and slopped a man's shirt over it, moving the shirt hard, as if trying to grate it. She did not glance up at her mother, who was moving on to the next task. The floor where her mother stood was spotless. What a shabby way to live! With little jobs lined up like shells that a person had to shatter with gunfire, one by one! Elena closed her eyes. Her skin throbbed. Her hands were pale from being so much in water, but they were not shrinking. They were puffing up, like dead creatures.

She heard a ukulele playing out on Beef Street.

Come in here, she ordered the sounds. Come in here, and

wrap yourself around my hands. My fat dead hands. I'm Ukulele's daughter. I deserve some of what that instrument can do and some of its good fortune.

She waited, scrubbing the shirt.

"Help me pour this out, Elena," said her mother, holding up a pail of dirty water, and another task interceded.

But the next day, she recognized the shirt she had been scrubbing. A man came into the laundry wearing it and said, "Did you wash and iron this?"

Elena nodded.

"Thank you! Thank you! You know, I've had a chest cold for a week, and the moment I put this shirt on, I was cured!" he said.

Amelia looked up from her ironing board. "That's nice," she said curtly.

"Yes, it is!" he said. He grasped Elena's hands, and though she tried to pull them away, he would not let go. He did not seem to notice how huge they were.

"Thank you," she said, as the man backed out of the laundry, so that he could gaze at her the entire time he retreated.

"Well, what was that about?" asked her mother.

"I'm not sure," said Elena, but within a week, the people in Honolulu, and out on the sugar and pineapple fields, and encircling the Punchbowl's slopes, were comparing stories about the Vasconcellos Laundry. One old lady put on a skirt ironed by Elena, and could do cartwheels. She did them down the center of Emma Street. A man claimed that when he unwrapped his shirts and inhaled their fragrance, his sinuses cleared and were lined with what he swore was a scent of gardenias. When people wiped their foreheads with a Vasconcellos-ironed handkerchief, their headaches left them. A priest who had sent in his collars to be starched preached the best sermon of his life. People heading for the beaches and sharing their talk-stories would suddenly burst into song and execute some dance steps, which startled them, until they remembered that they were carrying towels that had been sent to the Vasconcellos Laundry.

Throughout the air, excitement was stretched like a string.

Elena kept her hands in the water, and neither she nor her

mother knew that the one incident with the shirt had grown into a commotion until the morning that a servant from Ainahau came in and said that her mistress, Kaiulani, had heard about the laundress who made the cloth she touched more lively, the cloth that was causing all this singing and dancing in Honolulu, and she wanted to try it. The servant explained that Kaiulani was a sickly young girl, and any service rendered on her behalf would be appreciated. She spent much of her time out in her garden, hoping the air and her flowers would give her strength, but she needed some extra help.

The servant looked first at Elena and then at Amelia, and said, "Which of you has the touch?"

"What insanity—" Amelia began, but paused. The woman did seem to be from the royal family. An impressive carriage waited on Beef Street.

Elena paused, and glanced at her mother.

"It's my mother," said Elena. Giving her mother the credit was unrehearsed, and as startling to her as it was to Amelia. Elena was gratified to see that in some far recess of her heart, when called upon, she wanted her mother to shine. A momentary pleasure crossed Amelia's face.

"Yes," she said.

The servant handed over some cotton dresses with elaborate trims, and a velvet one with bows.

"They'll be ready tomorrow," said Amelia.

The servant said she looked forward to Kaiulani's dancing in her garden.

Amelia, not speaking to Elena, washed the dresses with the fine white powdered soap that they saved for undergarments. Elena could feel how carefully her mother was going over every button shank, every eyelet. She used a horsehair brush against the grain of the velvet. Elena was waiting to be called over, for her mother at least to say thank you or let her touch the princess's clothing. Only the sound of Amelia's anxious motions filled the laundry. Elena comforted herself. She was the one with ukulele powers inside her hands, a containment of the titanic sweeping event enacted by her father when he brought a new kind of music to a new country—it was under her fingers, within her, by surprise.

When she offered to iron Kaiulani's dresses and her mother declined, Elena was annoyed. Did her mother expect ukulele strains to get into the clothes without Elena's hands on them?

The servant pulled up in the carriage the next day, and Amelia gave her the dresses in packages tied up with white ribbons. Elena stayed in the back room, putting cream on her hands to soften them.

After she and her mother began their walk home that evening, they passed several young women forming a human pyramid, teasing one another as they tumbled over, and an old Hawaiian was doing a can-can number. He might have gone to the Barbary Coast and come scurrying home. The birds-of-paradise along the roadway pointed their beaks skyward, laughing.

"Mama," said Elena. "What's going on in Hawaii?"

Her mother looked at her, then away. Elena knew why. It was too much to think that lone acts of ironing, as innocent as playing a ukulele, could bring a giddiness to strangers.

But once she had allowed her ukulele powers to go into the world at large, that world began to report back to her what it was doing and seeing. She heard that the Portuguese were not alone in grumbling about Kalakaua being in the pocket of Claus Spreckels, the German sugar man, who was providing the king with huge personal loans and convincing him to arrange for more low-paid Japanese workers.

There was a rumor about the whites, some of them *haoles* and some the native-born sons of the missionaries, pressuring the king into redrafting the constitution, so that only property owners could vote. That would prevent many native Hawaiians from having a say in the government. The whites wanted America to annex the islands.

Her father came home at hours when neither she nor her mother were conscious, to sleep on the couch. Right under their noses, right under their eyes, he was turning into a memory.

Kaiulani's servant returned to the laundry one morning, and both Elena and her mother looked up eagerly. The royal account was going to be theirs!

"I am to deliver a message," said the servant.

Elena turned off her iron, and Amelia dried her hands on her apron. "Yes!" said Amelia. "I know the princess has many dresses, but we're never too overworked to—"

"I am to say," said the servant, "that Princess Kaiulani is having nervous fits. She is so anxious that she went into her garden and uprooted some of the prettiest hibiscus plants, rare ones, before her father could stop her. I don't know why you would bring gladness to everyone else, and destruction to her."

"I don't think—" began Amelia.

"I've heard that her governess is leaving her to get married," interrupted Elena. "That would explain the trouble."

"No matter what is going on in the life of the princess," said the servant, "your laundry was supposed to aid her. It did not. It has had the opposite effect. I fear the happiness in the streets must be short-lived. Likelike, the mother of the princess, is recommending that no one visit your store. I'm sorry." She lowered her voice. "I truly am sorry. I never believed the stories I was hearing. They seemed out of some fantasy."

"Which is what my daughter lives in," said Amelia, her hands shaking. "Just like her father. She's the one who should have done the work, and she didn't."

The servant and her mother were looking at Elena, who stared at her mother in helpless fury.

"Weren't you the one with the touch?" asked the servant.

"My daughter said that because she gets lazy about doing her work. Look at the pile of things behind her."

The servant peered at Elena. "You didn't want to help the princess?" she asked.

"You said you didn't believe what you were hearing," said Elena, her voice controlled.

"I'm here to deliver a message. I've done that. Now, if you'll excuse me." The servant headed back to the waiting carriage, but she turned at the door and said, "I do wish you well, myself. I wanted it to be true."

"Mother," said Elena, and was speechless. Her mother had returned to her ironing. For fear of bursting out screeching, Elena hid in the storeroom, and stared at the piles of unwashed clothes

with loathing. There did not seem to be much of a point in cleaning them, not if business was going to fall off and die. She did not
know why it had not occurred to her that her mother was jealous.
The ukulele had given Frank a place at court, and it had bestowed
wonder upon Elena, but it had granted nothing to Amelia. Nothing except grief that her husband was never around—or was that
its gift to her? Nothing more than she deserved!

And yet, Elena remembered being a child and her mother
teaching her how to make strudel: How to use the backs of one's
hands to stretch the dough that they draped over the table. This
was to teach Elena patience. Whenever she tore the dough, her
mother would tell her to slow down—and she did, her hands like
large turtles under the thin pale yellow sheets.

Hesitating to curse her own mother, no matter what she had
done, Elena prayed silently that Likelike and Kaiulani should have
music enter their hearts and beat so fast that their bodies exploded.
How dare they complain about their laundry! How dare they insist
upon magic, and condemn her for not providing it! Once made,
her prayer could not be taken back. She prayed it again to prevent
herself from directing anything against her mother.

During the failing days of the laundry, Frank brought his
daughter to a party at the garden of Ainahau. He wore a linen suit,
and was so formal with her that she did not recognize him.

"How is your mother, Elena?" he asked as they stood in a
corner of the lawn, watching the people dressed in silks and the
women in feather headdresses. There were many white men with
white beards, like Archibald Cleghorn.

She was wearing the boots that pinched more than ever, now
that she was doing the last of her growing. She wanted her father
to introduce her to his new friends and not keep her off to the
side. "You could find out for yourself, Daddy."

"I come home."

"When we're asleep."

He picked up his ukulele and tested the strings. Elena saw King
Kalakaua and ran toward him. He might lift the ban on bringing

clothes to the Vasconcellos Laundry! After all, he was the one in charge, not Likelike. When she got close enough to him to speak, though, she stared at him in dismay. He was drunk and very old, with gray in his beard.

"Your Highness?" she said, hating how timid she sounded. "Remember me? Ukulele's daughter?"

He was in red and gold, the royal colors, and was drinking from a tumbler. He splashed a little on her as he said, "Who? Whose daughter?" He stared over her head at the groups of men scattered throughout the garden. The breeze was light, but carrying muffled sounds.

Elena looked from him to her father, who was strolling through the gardens, playing his ukulele. But the music had become common enough to linger in the background and remain there, and no one was turning to applaud. Her father had made himself a jester, a minstrel; but better that than a luna in a cane field, better to be in a place where the trees and flowers had been brought in for their calming influence on a daughter. Before she ran out, Elena saw Kaiulani wearing a European-style dress with a sailor's collar and thick black stockings. Her black hair curled down to her shoulders, and she had on a white ginger lei, the kind worn by brides. She stood with some friends, but like the king, her Papa Moi, she seemed to be barely listening to them. She had a very old spirit.

Kaiulani spotted Elena and waved. Elena, thunderstruck, waved back. *Hello, my friend, we're these children with old spirits and long histories and new music springing around us, and no idea of what to do with any of it.*

I take back the curse I put on her, I take it back, I take it back, thought Elena as she ran from the party, not telling her father good-bye. If only she could have a second chance to iron Kaiulani's dress. She would have the ukulele powers make Kaiulani do handsprings.

Surely her prayer against the princess and Likelike, since it had been silent and haphazard, would not count.

Likelike died first. Not many servants knocked out their teeth in mourning, since Likelike had been so ill-tempered with many of them. The rumor arrived, while Elena and her mother sat in the laundry waiting for the occasional person to drift in, that the king had prayed her to death. Kalakaua himself, using his powers to kill someone in his own family! His own sister! The white people were not going to help him stay on the throne, and the sugar magnates were angling to control the constitution, and the king, so the story went, had to turn to the gods. They were demanding a sacrifice from the royal family, and he chose to doom his sister.

Likelike went sad but resigned to her bed, and caught a fever. Before dying, she blurted at Kaiulani that she would never be queen.

Elena fell sick herself. The king had not been acting alone with his bad prayers. No one knew that but her. She had cursed Likelike, and Kaiulani as well! That in one angry moment something could glide across her thoughts and assist in pulling down a family was awful beyond anything she had done.

I take it back, she prayed, I take it back. Every morning for two years when she awoke, she called back the powers of what she had wished.

When Kaiulani was sent off to school in England, Elena thought of warm things, so that the princess would not be chilled. She pictured Kaiulani in wool coats and mufflers, and the fervor of these prayers made Elena's body grow and her hands shrink to meet it. They were normal. As uneventfully as that. Now that they were in proportion to the rest of her, now that people seldom brought in anything for her or her mother to iron, her hands were so ordinary as to be repellent to her.

One night when she and Amelia were alone at home, her mother said, while washing the dishes and handing them to Elena to dry, "How nice to see your problem is gone, darling."

"Gone?" said Elena. Her mother had never called her darling before. How distasteful, to be loved because she was no longer a freak. "I'll tell you what's gone, Mama," she said, continuing to dry her mother's dinner plate, "and that's Daddy. Don't you care?"

Her mother did not pause in scrubbing another plate. "No, I don't," she said. "If I care, he wins."

"He wins what?"

"I don't expect you to understand."

"I might surprise you. Maybe I'll surprise you the way I did our old customers."

"Don't start with that nonsense." She slammed a plate hard onto Elena's hand.

"Ouch. I don't know why you have to be so mean, Mama."

"You don't have to worry about us getting divorced. I'll never give him a divorce! Never! You understand me?" She was facing her daughter, and shouting. "All I wanted was not to be one of those old spinsters! Those awful women! You want to be one of them? Do you?" She shattered a dish on the floor, and Elena understood that her mother was doing it to cover the crashing sound of the thought in her head: Elena was nothing but the thing had and done, so that her mother would not be one of those pathetic ladies who married, and discovered what love involved, and returned home to die. Elena was her mother's proof that she was not a lonely woman, that she had signed herself out of that grim club.

The king went for his first sleigh ride at the insistence of the mayor of Omaha, and caught a cold that lasted for the duration of his train trip across America.

Late into the rule of Kalakaua, Elena and her mother opened a new laundry and did moderately well. No wonderful stories, however, were reported about what they washed and ironed. Frank came by occasionally to give them money for their rent, and a divorce was never mentioned.

The king died in 1891, at the Palace Hotel in San Francisco, forced out by whites who made him sign the Bayonet Constitution, which gave them the upper hand in the rules of state.

In 1897, Kaiulani took to her bed with a headache in Paris, electing not to attend a bazaar. That afternoon, a booth at the bazaar caught fire, a ceiling collapsed, and 117 people died. Her chronic illness had spared her.

She was coming home to Hawaii. Though a provisional gov-

ernment led by missionaries' children and sugar plantation owners had kicked out the royal family, Kaiulani would return to her
garden and either rule from there or wait until this latest uproar
dissipated. With her aunt, Queen Liliuokalani, deposed and out
of the way, Kaiulani was first in line for the throne.

Elena thought this over with profound relief while leaning on
the counter of the laundry and pictured Kaiulani lying wan in bed
but smiling at the manner fate had chosen to spare her. Her hair
would blow in the breeze as she rolled through the streets of
Honolulu in her phaeton, to the welcoming cries of the crowd.

Elena would go to her, wave at a respectful distance, and say,
Your eyes met mine, do you remember, in your garden, when
neither of us understood what the adults were doing. Let me help
you continue the ways of your father. Let my hands wash music
into whatever wraps around you.

This did not happen for the princess, nor for Elena.

Kaiulani returned to Hawaii and was forced to while away her
time at Ainahau. History could permeate the air as soundly as
music. The Americans were moving in, and the kingdom seemed
permanently pried away from the royal inheritors. Elena thought
of Kaiulani and her retinue of peacocks watching the gardeners
tending her trees, hoping that some upset would clear the path to
the throne for her.

Frank continued to play at society parties, and Elena and her
mother saw him infrequently. On one occasion they spotted him
through the open doorway of a bar, surrounded by women. One
had her arm draped over him. The others were clapping as he
strummed a ukulele. Amelia stared toward him. He did not see
her or Elena out on the sidewalk.

"Mama, let's go," said Elena, tugging her mother's arm.

Her mother's face went soft and white as cotton.

"Mama."

Her mother ran, her head down, pushing through the crowd.
She bumped into people, who shoved her back.

"Mama!" called Elena.

Her mother was wearing a loose Mother Hubbard, and as she
ran she stumbled forward, her toe hitting a tuft of grass thrusting

itself through the sidewalk, and she fell and hit her head on the pavement.

"Mama, Jesus, Mama," said Elena, turning her mother over and seeing blood seep from her crown. She cradled her mother's head and screamed for help. That fast it had come, this accident so long in the making.

She prayed that her hands would grow hideously large again. If they had at one time made cloth breathe life into strangers, then it was reasonable to expect that large hands, if pressed against her mother's head, would cause life to flow into it. That was what took place, as Elena wished it. Her hands grew, she held her mother's head with them, and Amelia stayed alive. She brought tea to her mother, and ran the laundry by herself, and when her father brought flowers, Elena asked him to leave and take his useless flowers with him. She lay the big palms of both hands onto her mother's head when she had headaches, and they left her quickly, although she had become odd and daft and so relaxed that she scarcely knew who she was.

When Amelia was better and able to walk by herself, Elena wished her big hands gone, but they would not go. She soaked them for hours in the hottest water she could stand, but they stayed with her, even when she cried and pleaded for them to vanish.

Please, please, she prayed every night. They'll make me an old maid. If they don't shrink, I will never be able to be Hawaiian and step out naked to greet the dawn after my wedding night.

Tragedy struck during Elena's pleadings with her hands. Kaiulani, at the age of twenty-three, caught cold during a rainstorm and died. Something as dull as being rained upon! For lack of a warm garment, a line had ended. There were no more heirs to the throne. Elena grieved that her curse should be summoned up, but she was also afraid to cry out that it had actually been intended for her mother. That curse had been so offhanded, during a small, private moment—and for it to come to this!

It chilled her that there was no act, no matter how furtive, that did not impose itself upon the enormous backdrop of events. If anyone attempted to hide, then history would come in and envelop the smallest person in the smallest corner.

While feeding her mother her cereal, Elena realized that the curse had been much smarter than she could imagine. It knew that she had not meant to bring harm to Kaiulani or Likelike, but to her mother. Therefore here her mother was, alive but disabled by a fall. She was as easily enamored as a child. She drummed her hands on the tabletop when Elena cut up a banana. Amelia never had to comb her hair or sweep floors or worry. She did not have to feel like a woman petrified of the future.

Caring for her elderly mother was a full time job, and even if Elena had normal hands, it was unlikely that she would find a husband. She would be her mother—or rather her mother as her mother would have continued—growing old in a panic.

Elena hung a portrait of Kaiulani in the halls.

"Pretty girl! Pretty girl!" sang Amelia. "Amen!"

"That's Kaiulani, Mama," she said.

"O! O!"

Elena would keep Kaiulani nearby, as a reminder that one could have a whole life planned out, a job assigned from birth, a garden with imported trees, and there was still no guessing how fast the earth could change, how indistinct the most familiar people could grow, how casually a curse or rebellion could fester, how a rainstorm or a fall or quirk of birth could scramble history, how untidily power could grow in one's grasp, though it might vibrate prettily as a string concerto.

Hardly more than a decade later, Elena put her mother in a wheelchair and went out to see the tearing up of the gardens of Ainahau to make room for a hotel. The peacocks had been sold and some of the salvageable plants given away for low prices at an auction. The legislature had decided that royal tokens were no longer of much interest, not since the United States had made Hawaii a territory. Archibald Cleghorn had died, and though he had worked to dedicate the garden for public use, the legislature voted against its upkeep.

Elena tucked a blanket up higher, near her mother's chin. She ironed everything, including blankets, to fill her days, hoping some of the ukulele power would return.

"Nurse," said her mother. "What are they doing? Let's go home!"

"I'd like to watch," said Elena. "It's a place where a princess used to live. I thought one day we would live in a place like that. You and I would have a garden that was like that one over there. Because Daddy seemed to be making lots of money. He brought a new kind of music here. And for a while, my hands did amazing things."

"How nice!"

"Not so nice, actually, Mama." The breeze was lifting the palm leaves on the trees as men with pickaxes headed into the estate to pull up what remained of the garden. A wrecking ball was set up near the house.

"O! What's that noise?"

"They're taking down the house, Mama. No one lives there anymore."

"No, no," said Amelia. "Not that noise! Not that noise! I'm hearing something else!"

Elena sighed, and could picture Kaiulani observing the end of her history, and Hawaii's history. If only she could turn her gaze upon Elena with her infirmed mother, to see that the story of the ukulele family, a history that had begun not long ago as an adjunct to royal dreams, was also at something of an end. Now the strings were invisible, and the garden would be tossed here and there, so that even the ghosts would not find it.

"Are you hearing a ukulele, Mama?" she asked. "A *braguinha*? Is it your stomach singing?"

"Shh! Shh, nurse!" said her mother. "Lord Almighty! Listen!"

That is what I shall do, thought Elena. I shall hold up my burdensome hands, and the moment I identify the song on the wind, it will pass on, leaving me to listen for the next one.

The harmony behind each of those songs will be constant. It will be: Plant no gardens; plant no gardens. A trousseau has no merit. Every plan is cursed, the heedless way we live now.

ADD
BLUE TO
MAKE
WHITE
WHITER

#1

Mamãe said, "Come watch." I pulled a chair over to the stove. Then I was tall enough to see clearly. Into the boiled icing she squeezed a drop of blue coloring. The blue swirled into a gyre and then disappeared. The icing went from flat oyster white to heavenly white, as if not blue but the absence of blue had been added. What a fabulous discovery, that consuming an opposite makes something more itself! I clapped my hands. "Be careful," warned Mamãe. "If you overdo, you'll have a blue mess you'll have to throw out."

One day my Tia Alma went overboard with bluing on her yellowed hair. Instead of turning lovely spun white, she was aqua. I laughed. Usually she went around saying out loud what everyone had done wrong, as she ticked off the decades on her rosary's hard little beads. She was a *beata* who prayed for us to clean ourselves up. Now she was wrecked and had to hide in her house.

#2

Sister Dominique Delgado kept us after school whenever we missed the morning bell. She taught us to be on time by deepening our day into more lateness. Sometimes her eyes had no pupils. For extra penance, so that she would attain eternal happiness,

Sister wore dark sweaters in the heat and prayed the Rosary with arms outstretched on an invisible cross. We followed her example until we were wearing anchors in our lungs and on our shoulders.

Sister explained the Redemption. "God so loved us that His only Son's life was poured out for our sins," she said. Christ shed His blood so that we would end our bloodletting ways.

Sister Dominique Delgado lost me with this salvation talk. How did condemning His own Son prove that God loved us? Christ was spotless, and we are made of mud. We dissolve so easily. It should be harder for God to like us, although that is none of our doing. How could death win us everlasting life, especially if we too must die? I got slapped for saying that being left with death as a ticket was a lousy bargain.

But this I can see: Christ was an ultimate in love; to die of it— He shines, shines. Into his pure act, the world has been steadily dripping blood. We have made the world too red.

#3

Joe and I fell in love. Nothing quenched our desire: I arched like a cat when his kisses grazed my spine. I tried swallowing his tongue. He lost his fingers to the knuckle inside me.

He worked in the dairy, and sometimes I helped him pour blue bleach into the wash to keep his uniforms perfect. I did this cleaning for myself, too, to maintain in my house the smell of bleach that reminded me of him.

Stop, friends warned me over drinks. You are whirling out of control. He will never leave his wife.

I would nod and motion for another round.

You are not yourself, they would whisper.

I wish, I wish! Aren't all of us dying to leave ourselves and enter the edifice of someone else. Lost in the opposing man, the opposing woman, we finally find ourselves one mortal cathedral. And inside—carnelian lamps. The world has appointed three places where a red light must burn: near every tabernacle, in parlors of nameless love, and in roads where people must stop.

When I quit seeing Joe, he came to me more than ever. In a

dream he perched on a roof and dropped eggs toward me as I stood on the ground. Eggshells are models of expert housing, but are imperfectly fragile. I had to catch the eggs, or they would explode into a snotty yellow around my feet. Several had straw pasted onto them with old barnyard shit, and I wanted to talk to him about rinsing them off. "Joe?" I said, looking up. "A moment, wait just a moment," he said, but he was not waiting, not glancing at me. More eggs fell, right through my hands. Then I woke up.

When I was alone, his laurel and salt taste would seep into my throat. I stopped washing my clothes, because the smell of bleach, all confused with him, was killing me. I found old seminal glue with trapped hair on the top of my desk, like lashes held in resin. Bedclothes held up to the light had sweat shaped like storybook animals—cats, a flying bear, the neck of a giraffe, and in dead center always some wet radiance I christened what was missing, my Joseph.

I wound my sheet around myself, but I never slept. An unseen choir sang in my room at night. (I could see no one anymore.) Over and over in the melody was the word *refrain, refrain,* a word containing its own opposites: *Stay away, hold back, refrain;* and at the same time *fall into the same thing, repeat it at intervals.* This music made me dazed. I moved to another apartment, because I could no longer live without him. My plan was to stack up enough empty weeks in a new place, and then I would be cured. On that glorious Blank Day I could declare, He lived, but that was ages ago and far away. I am clean! He is not the underside of my life.

#4

To fix a wine hangover, I simply drank more wine. Beer also worked, but the bottles clanked like the sound of a Chinese lion dance when I carried them to the trash. Hello, Tia Alma! This? Yes, what a feast it was. What else did I learn while doing my best to erase everything I knew? A Headache Law: Beware of Frangelico, Amaretto, Frambrosia. Those formulas of the monks laced my head with sugar spiders. The more I drank, the more I expected less to be inside me, but eventually there were many nestfuls of these sugar creatures. A Dream Law: One can live a long time alone with spiders. A Law of Losing, Fuzzily, One's Boundaries: The air hurt my skin, which became rough and fly-away, like asbestos. My whole body was trying to escape from me, and it was easiest for my skin to turn into fibers that were light as a dream. I wished my skin well, sincerely, as it floated off. He had kissed every cell of it, and I knew it was going away to search for him. I had always wanted to watch him unnoticed, to understand how he could exist in a place where I was not. A Recovery Law: I stopped talking about him. But time does not lessen anything; it adds and adds. My friends said, *congratulations, we knew you would get over it*. So I had them fooled. I wore the hours like stripping bandages, winding them around me from head to foot, because I had drunk away my skin. People had been too polite to mention the missing skin, and now they did not point out that I was a mummy. I worked at a switchboard for the phone company, day after day, never getting to listen in, and I won a plaque for perfect attendance. It served as a hot-plate. I was waiting hopefully for my skin to return with its report, but it would never be mine again.

#5

I told myself, very sternly, that the time had come to grow a new skin. I pulled off one bandage after another, but within each one there was a faint dampness of some memory. My head itched as I unwound it, and reaching up, to my horror, I discovered red sugar spiders running through my hair. The damage caused in me by the Amaretto had reproduced. The spiders sang, "Funiculi, Funicula," and slaughtered "A Te O Cara," chuckling because their voices were terrible. No new skin was forming to keep me solid. I was a sponge without calcium, and sank down, clutching my head, then shaking off the spiders that scampered over my hands. I crawled outside for the garden hose to melt them.

"*O! Basta! Basta!*" they cried, but without mercy I flooded the water over them. Soon I was floating in the little lagoon I had made from killing the red sugar spiders. I could sense almost at once my terrible error. The spiders were dissolved in the lagoon, but I was a sponge and soaked them up. They suffused every part of me. I was a body full of broken spiders.

Frogs swarmed around to buoy me up. "Thank you," I said. Their warty leader was smiling. "Allow us," he said. "Fine," I answered him, "but tell me, why are all of you blue?" Turning a round eye toward me, he croaked, "My dear, because you're blue, and we want to keep you company. Don't you know that? Don't you know anything? Blue, blue," he sang stupidly. "Rrk! Rrk!" his blue minions laughed, and started biting. I screamed. Of course! They were after the fine spun sugar I was carrying thoroughly within. My arms and legs were heavy, and the frogs held me down, knowing that my sense of fight was gone. Their horseshoe-shaped mouths sucked at me.

A large blue queen frog was waiting on a lily pad. She wore a shining gold crown and many rings that blinded my eyes with the sun they flashed. "Excellent," she sang. There was a pulp of me left, not difficult to drag to the queen's feet. I begged for her understanding. But this was a strange queen, with teeth. "Wring her out," she ordered.

They squeezed the liquid remaining in me into a thick-walled white bottle. I was dizzy. I smelled as if I were a pool, that high odor that evokes memories of childhood summers and notions of a painful cleanness that make the eyes smart. Then I felt it. I was bleach, which pours out blue to make things without mark or blemish. All that was remaining of me was concentrated into poisonous fumes, a cleanser that would cause skin rashes.

"I'll use you to wash my clothes and make them sparkle!" the queen rasped. *I'll fade your clothes,* I thought. *Wipe you clean away.* But I sat blue in the opaque bottle, knowing that she would be controlling the measure of me poured. I would come out in a pale stream, not even a heavenly white, just enough to scrub away her dirt. She was dancing. I could feel the lily pad wobbling, tossing, as I stayed in my container. Her feet were going up and down, and the men were joining her; I was vibrating from being near frantic bodies, without any of the motions being mine. Tia Alma was choking with laughter.

Certainly I was sloshing a bit, but that is not dancing, most assuredly not. I would have to wait indefinitely for cleaning day, when the bleach bottle of me would be employed in proper cupfuls, until it was empty. I would find myself nostalgic for the days of the Italian spiders, when I could hope for a sweet web to cling to.

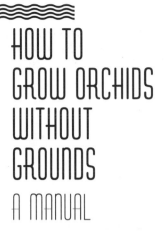

HOW TO
GROW ORCHIDS
WITHOUT
GROUNDS
A MANUAL

Orchids are a psychological puzzle: No other plant has as many species, which implies a certain resiliency, and yet their delicacy, coupled with their suggestion of the tropics, makes them quite . . . feared.

On 26 August at 5:35 A.M., in Lodi in north central California, according to the police report, orchids were found at the home of George and Maria Luisa Sousa and their four children. The orchids hung on three small bark slabs nailed high on the rec room wall, which George had recently fitted with inexpensive paneling to reduce outside noise. He informed Officer James MacMillan that he was often incapable of sleeping to a decent hour, but that he had noticed no commotion out of the ordinary. The heating had been turned up, but nothing else was awry. The temperature had made the baby colicky and his wife sleepy, but no one was seriously harmed. All very strange, George and MacMillan concluded, not certain what crime the intruder had committed. George, a Vietnam veteran, was able to spot the path where a man who obviously knew what he was doing had, by hand, bent the grass blades back into place to cover his footprints. It was clearly a man, on account of the shape and depth of the imprints. George first discovered the trail not by sight, but because the whitening hairs on his arms were standing and pointing toward that particular path.

What kinda strange flowers don't like the earth, said Mac-

Millan, glaring at the orchids on the bark patches. Nor was he sure what to think of roots that crawled like white worms right near the blooms, like those horrible things his wife now insisted on putting in salad; what were they? Bean sprouts. Anyhow salad was not food fit for a man who was stuck working day and night with people, who were made out of meat, did George agree?

I don't know, said George. I don't know how to take care of them, and there's no place to put water that I can figure, so I guess we'll leave them where they are and hope they live on just air. If they don't they'll die and we'll put them in the compost. Jesus. I don't know how come, but my oldest boy, Daniel, he's eight, cried when he saw them but wasn't about to let me take them down. I said make up your mind what bothers you, and then change it, but he's the sort of kid who'll stop and stand in the rain because he's afraid if he runs through more rain to get to a shelter, he'll get even wetter. I don't know what to do for him. You got kids, Jim?

Doesn't sound like you know very much, said MacMillan, but if I had a boy like that I'd keep a watch on him real close. You got any breakfast steaks in the house, and honest-to-God cream? Damn, man, it's still hot in here and I'm starving, you got a wife who throws out every decent thing in the world? No more animal products, says her royal highness. I say when you get to be our age eating's our number one way to grab part of the world and own it, am I right?

If you say so. I don't eat so much myself.

Then you won't mind if I help myself a little to your fried eggs.

Or whatever's upstairs. Come on. I can hear the coffee.

You can what?

Hear the coffee. Percolating. I love that sound. Makes me feel like it's cold outside and warm inside and that I'm home, smelling something that's like the ground of a jungle but safe, and all together it's some new lease on life.

You must get alotta headaches. How'd you learn to hear weird like that?

I learned. Come on upstairs.

Officer MacMillan bounded up the stairs ahead of him. Smelled like bacon, what luck. His job description included never showing fear, people fell over like dominos if you did that, but those flowers on the wall gave him more than the usual creeps that flowers had a habit of throwing at him. Flowers pretended to be watching you but they never had any eyes. Those ones on the wall had loony open mouths like something he wasn't supposed to look at.

Epiphytic orchids—that is, ones that grow off the ground and are air-nourished, sometimes cleverly hidden in trees—as well as terrestrials must be watched with care; a fungus or pest can consume them overnight. "Slab cultures" attached to cork or fern barks replicate epiphytic orchids as they are found in nature, with plenty of free air circulation to prevent rotting.

Afonso tapped the clay pot, loosening the fresh seedlings of a *Catasetum macrocarpum*. These orchids were bright green with yellow lips, and the red spots on them were numerous and healthy. Using a fine brush he removed every trace of the osmunda potting mix from the roots and wrapped some galvanized wire around them to form a ball that he attached to a piece of bark padded with ferns. Bark was such an interesting background, shaped with an involved perimeter, like the boundaries of a country when no one could decide on its government. This would be for the O'Connell's house. In a week he would need to return and cut away the wires, once the roots knew they were expected to grip the bark. He yawned. He was tired from waiting last night for the sisters at Mount Carmel Convent to finish their late offices, although breaking into the convent and attaching orchids along the corridors had gone like a charm.

From his greenhouse the world outside looked pale and green.

The stomatas, or leaf pores, permanently gape open; this is a quality that sets orchids apart from all other flowers. This is why they like the humidity, as they cannot control their weeping.

Maria Luisa knew her disappointment was not Officer MacMillan's fault, but she resented feeding him. Here she was thinking—hoping—the orchids in the rec room were a surprise from

George. He used to be like that, and then bang, that fast, that's not it at all. It's some florist terrorist act, and here's Jim, who's got uniform complex: give him a suit and a gun, and he'll get into the middle of things but never muster anything that needs doing. She had cut circles out of the toast with a cookie cutter and fried the eggs in the middle, like they did at that café in Lisbon where she and George had gone the year after his arm healed. So romantic! She had not minded seeing the cigarette butts, thousands of them like spent cartridges, in the crevices of the cobblestones. All she had noticed in Lisbon was that George finally looked happy.

Now it turned out those orchids downstairs weren't from him, and he wasn't eating the eggs in their toast frames, and Jim Mac-Millan was. Imagine, asking if she wouldn't mind being a doll— Jim had actually said that, and instead of defending her, George was busy forcing himself to swallow a spoonful of Deidre's cereal—would she be a *doll* and make him another one of "them egg things." God, it's a wonder he didn't say, "rustle me up . . ." Jim had no right to look at her as if she were a fallen woman, his eyes with angry pointedness not looking below her collarline, just because she was in her robe at nine o'clock. For his information, she had to go to Daniel's school and explain why her son only drew monsters' hands during art hour, and she did not want to sweat on her dress until the last possible minute.

I'm gonna catch him, said George.

Catch whom? said Maria Luisa, looking at Jim, who didn't seem to care.

That fellow.

Maria Luisa sat up. Maybe he thought she had an admirer. Come to think of it, maybe she *did* have one. Mr. Bettencourt, the rancher? Handsome but too rough. God, he made his own boots right off the backs of his livestock and was proud of it. She thought of the animals screaming. Maybe jealousy would bring George back to her; she'd take bad motives, if it turned out all right in the end. Sometimes strange gifts worked out for the best.

I know he's coming back because he left his scent here, said George, and no one who lays down that inner spray of himself can stay away forever.

Like I said, you must get alotta headaches, real bangers, said Officer MacMillan, wiping a crust of toast over the spilled canary yellow egg on his plate.

Maria Luisa cleared Jim's plate right as he grabbed for the last corner of toast. Before going to Daniel's school, she would play the cassette of *fados* her Titia Néné Calheiros sent her from Lisbon: the songs that often suggested what a bursting heart would sound like, if the sound could be magnified. Many of them were about women who thought they would never see their husbands again.

One effect of that particular war was that the greenhouses of England were bombed along with other buildings, and many orchids were shipped for safety to the United States, which has never known, incidentally, any foreign invasion. The English were told to grow vegetables and arguably less beautiful but more practical things such as Afonso also grew, lettuce, carrots for better eyesight, and potatoes with their eyes watching him from their graves. His hope was one day to live without ever leaving his house, although he knew this was a childish and false dream about the nature of security. In fact deep in his heart, where he also stored the picture of that girl screaming for help (that even more than the image of the men around him blooming into fire), he understood that he was planting orchids in people's homes so that he would have a reason to stay in motion. Orchids required a lot of tending, and though they could live a long while on air, he would have to check them occasionally. It could get very complicated, this business of breaking into places and leaving without being seen. Not that being caught would be so terrible. But it would alter the game, which was to surprise with corsages as many people as possible, without inviting their nagging need to feel obligated, until it felt as if he had dispensed orchids to the world at large. He was dying to be a teenager back home in Lisbon again, walking along the banks of the Tejo with Leonor wearing a corsage. If the world were going to accept him back, after what he had done, he would have to court it first, like a gentleman.

He wiped a drop of water off the column of a white cattleya with a green throated interior, an *Epidendrum mariae* "Doris"— there were so many tribes to memorize. Even a single water spot could trigger the death of the whole plant. He loved and admired that about orchids: Something as simple as a drop of water could change them forever. Such a little thing (what everyone else might call little) could make living impossible!

He was out of light meters, which needed to be installed at the Bettencourt ranch, which he had broken into last week. That meant a visit to the hardware store, which was so wonderful with its smell of peat, its filtered light, and that mystical way that everyone entering the garden center suddenly walked more softly.

The units of measure to determine the proper intensities of light for orchids are called "foot candles." Most orchids will thrive within a 1,500–4,000 foot-candle range—but wait a minute! Thrive? Even with the most scrupulous care, the best blooms will only last a month or two, perhaps twice a year. The rest of the time, the leaves are, frankly, dull. It is a testimony to the glory of orchids that we patiently await their rare blooms.

It was not that Daniel did not try, explained Sister Angela, whose face glowed with high color. She was a kind woman, and therefore did not blame her students for being too young to appreciate that kindness. Some children blossomed under certain conditions, while others would not find the proper strength of inspiration until they were older. Daniel was well-behaved. Did he have nightmares? Some trouble at home, though she knew Maria Luisa and George were good parents? Could there be an explanation for Daniel's drawing monster hands?

May I see one of his pictures? asked Maria Luisa.

Certainly.

Sister Angela looked through a stack of butcher-paper drawings, with their lines and swaths of tempera paint cracking. The hands Daniel had painted were crabbed and hairy, with huge claws. At least they were floating, not attacking anything.

Well, said Maria Luisa. I'll say this. As monster hands go, they're pretty good. Don't you think, Sister?

They're not bad. Sister held them at arm's length and nodded.

Then I don't think we have a problem here, do you?

Not yet, Mrs. Sousa, but I worry.

Until we know what his problem is, I don't think there's much we can do. That's a lovely orchid, Sister.

Sister Angela pointed to the cattleya, yellow and bright, pinned to the front of her long black scapular. I found it this morning, she said, in the hallway outside my room. It's so pretty!

Yes, said Maria Luisa, ashamed that she was not depressed about Daniel, but about this news that she did not have a personal admirer. Not if Sister and everyone else had an orchid too. Large peninsulas of sweat spread out from the hollows beneath her arms. Being the recipient of some odd general goodwill was not nearly as breathtaking as singular ardor.

Orchids crave what is known as a "rest period," in which very little water is necessary. It is as if they are saying that the more gorgeous the bloom, the longer the weariness, which was the type that George felt as he wrapped a blanket around himself in the rec room: a weariness that marks waking time as half-sharp, without imparting rest.

Daniel came down the stairs and sat with him. I'm going to find him with you, Daddy, he said.

George let him crawl under the blanket. You mind telling me why?

I want to thank him. At first the flowers scared me, but that was only because I didn't know how they got there. Now I think they're really good.

They are great. He hugged Daniel closer.

Then why do you want to catch him, Daddy? Promise me you won't hurt him.

Is that what you think? That I'm going to hurt him?

I'm not sure. I don't think you'd do it to be mean.

I won't hurt him. I think you should stop listening to those kids at school telling you that soldiers are mad-dog killers. They're like you and me. I just want to ask him why he's going around planting orchids. That's the trouble today, Dan. We can say what's going on but we don't wait for the why of it to come to us. Like, for example, I know he was a soldier, but why flowers? Why orchids?

How do you know he was a soldier, Daddy? Daniel thought the

kids at school would shut up with their torture about his father being crazy and say he was smart, if they could hear this.

I know it. I know it because a modern soldier learns that he is expected to make a mark so deep that he falls into it and disappears.

Oh, said Daniel, tucking his knees up to his chin, under the blanket, not sure he could remember this right for the school-ground. Or even if he should remember it. His father had a nice low voice but he never made much sense. Daniel wanted to thank the orchid man because everyone at school was talking about him instead of Daniel's father, for a change, and getting to talk to him before anyone else would be neat. Then he wouldn't be mad that the orchid man was going everywhere and not picking them out as special.

Rich men would send orchid hunters out into jungles, in search of what no other collectors had. Secrets about prize locations were carefully guarded, to protect specific corners of the market. Credit William Spencer Cavendish, the sixth Duke of Denvonshire, with making orchid growing a stylish pursuit. Isn't that always the case, rich men sending those without money into the dangers of the field!

Afonso stared at the young girl in her green apron behind the counter. She was about the same age as—he had to stop this. Unless he succeeded in forgetting that girl who was worlds away, years away, he would never be able to look anyone in the eye, especially women. His hands shook, and he hid behind a shelf of sprinklers and boxes of pest controls.

May I help you? he heard.

The panic was going to strangle him.

No, no, he said. No.

Are you ill? she asked. Do you need something?

Light meters.

He brushed the sweat off his forehead and raised his face to meet hers, then glanced away. She looked nothing like that Afri-can girl who had been lying trapped under his commanding offi-cer, but everywhere, especially in the eyes of young girls, Afonso saw a glimmer that could jump away from them at any second. He had stood there and not done a thing to help, and after the girl screamed, she had looked up, her body weighed down by another soldier who had not bothered to take off his muddy clothes. Afonso had been frozen. He thought he would never live long enough to move from that spot. He had always fancied himself an honorable man, possibly heroic. To punish him for his arrogance, and for freezing, the soul of the African girl rounded up like blisters over her eyes and popped and went away like steam. The girl lost her soul right in front of him.

After a third soldier got up, he said to Afonso, *Want some?*
Between the girl's legs was a pool of blood. She looked at him with dead eyes. They could not plead. He had fled.
He should at least have helped her up.
Oh, gosh, he thought, looking at the clerk in the gardening center. If only meanings would stay the same. Honestly, truly, he had been attempting to pin corsages everywhere, and now his gesture was getting complicated. Complicated because more than any other flower, orchids, with their languid richness, were how he could picture a soul looking; moist and with intense central designs. This was a very different matter, to be pinning the soul of that girl in everyone's home.
Sir?
I'm sorry. Sorry
For what? You said you wanted a light meter? What's that for?
Afonso hesitated. If he explained too much, she would know that he was the one giving people orchids.
I'll come back some other time, he said. He would drive into Modesto, where no one knew him, and ask there.
The girl smiled. *No offense, but you have a funny accent*, she said.
He told her that he was from Lisbon, originally, but that he had spent what seemed like forever in a place he could never say out loud, in Africa. It sounded like "angles," which amused him, because the land was open and smooth, so deceptively smooth that people felt compelled to go in and add their own points of resistance by fighting. He lived in California because it was a long way from Africa, and from Lisbon, where many men like him

wandered dazed because of the lands they had gone to not so long ago, in Africa.

Never heard of it, she smiled, smoothing down her green apron.

Never heard of it? He smiled back. It was wrong to expect the world to know completely what it had done. On the other hand, maybe he was putting up orchids because it horrified him that everyone did not know intimately of every terrible thing that had happened in the world, even faraway things.

You see something on the floor? she asked.

No, no, he said, still staring downward because he was not quite able to look right at her. It's just—you remind me of someone.

Mr. Sousa! Hello! she said.

Afonso turned around to see George Sousa holding his son Daniel's hand. The boy was staring at Afonso.

Afternoon, Teresa, said George. You're gonna have to explain to me how to take care of orchids. I'm at a loss. God. I feel like they're gonna die if I don't do everything just so.

I'm afraid of caring for them myself, Mr. Sousa, she said. I had some show up like mushrooms in my kitchen yesterday, and they stare at me. They're so bizarre that I don't look at them. Eventually they'll die but that's not my fault, now is it?

You could take them down, get rid of them? said George.

Afonso moved behind a high shelf, walking slowly toward the exit. George was eyeing him like he knew something, and so was his boy.

I could I suppose, said Teresa, but that might feel like outright murder, instead of letting them die and then throwing them out. That's sick too, but it doesn't make your hand in it as bad.

Afonso left the garden center; this was not the plan. Not the plan at all, to upset people. Unless those orchids really were the soul of the African girl multiplied, the soul pleading with everyone for help and understanding. Alas, for her and all victims, that would undoubtedly prove too much to behold.

Beginners have trouble understanding that an orchid may be killed with too much hesitant tenderness. For instance, the shock of a transplant is substantial, but it will be worse if the gardener does not pull the orchid out of its pot with authority and cut the plant into manageable sections. This seems so harsh to beginners that many of them unwittingly destroy healthy flowers through timidity.

They're not terrible! They're not! protested Sister Angela, the yellow cattleya quavering on her black scapular. She was not going to remove it until the Mother Superior absolutely ordered her to.

It gives me the vapors, thinking someone can get in here. We have no idea what this person is up to, said Sister Anselmo. Do we, Sister Angela? Really. This could be one of those strange murder cases where they leave the calling card first, and afterward we say, "Oh, my, we should have seen it coming."

If we're murdered in our beds, said Sister Angela, then I don't suppose we're going to be saying anything at all.

I plan to shout it in heaven, then, said Sister Anselmo crisply. She disliked the optimism Sister Angela displayed at inappropriate times.

That's enough, said Mother Pura, the Superior.

We could donate them to the children's hospital, suggested Sister Delfina.

The children's hospital! cried Sister Anselmo. Mark innocent children, for this murderer to go after! I shouldn't like to live with *that* on my conscience! Even if there's *someone* in this room who can't think that far ahead!

Sister Angela unpinned her cattleya, without waiting for Mother Pura's orders. The poor flower could feel the commotion. She cupped it in her hands and prayed for it. Mother Pura announced that they would care for the plants already there, but would request money from Father Marcello for extra locks to let the intruder know he was not welcome. Sister Angela felt the orchid shaking at the mere suggestion of a war.

A light coating containing malathion will prevent aphids and mealybugs from destroying orchids, though no matter how well-intentioned the grower is, outside forces can prove too much.

James MacMillan looked at the bowl in front of him and then shoved it angrily away. Hot liquid slopped over the lip of the bowl.

More white worms! Jesus Christ Almighty, he thought she'd already served him every goddamn food on the planet that looked like stuff that belonged in the ground, but no, no, what was this shit now?

Soba, she said.

What the fuck is that?

Soba noodles. They're Japanese. Please watch your language, Jim.

He stood and splashed the contents of the bowl into the sink, then slammed the bowl on the counter, not hard enough to break it—he worked hard to pay for the junk in this house—but hard enough for her to know he had had it up to here. Being hungry all the time could make any man insane.

Then ship it back to Japan, goddammit!

Jim. Please.

Better yet, you can go with it and open a goddamn capital A-robe-icks studio.

Jim.

She made him hate the sound of his own name. Jim, Jim, Jim, he was going crazy hearing his name from her and from everybody calling him about these break-ins. He had half a mind to shoot this orchid guy when he saw him. He had thrown out the ones he found in his garage. This stranger had gotten past the perimeter, but the day he crossed into James MacMillan's main camp, that was a day for drawing weapons and laying down the law. Throwing that flower in the trash had been a ripe delight, even with that wire booby trap wrapped around it.

As he headed for the Bettencourt Ranch, gunning his motor, MacMillan felt bands of muscles constricting in his back. Bettencourt felt the same as he did about some sneak coming onto his property like a coward in the dead of night, and there was a meeting tonight, because until something was done about this there was not going to be any peace anywhere.

The name orchid, *some say, stems directly from the Greek* orchis, *meaning testis, due to the shape of the roots. Others claim this is a fanciful and false assumption. Whatever the camp into which one falls, however, and whether or not one believes that Theophrastus and other ancient philosophers and scientists first described orchids in this way, it is quite true that in the old days people set out to determine the medicinal uses and character of the soul of a plant, based on what it looked like.*

Maria Luisa was pleased that she could finally name what troubled her about those orchids in the rec room. It was those red spots on the petals. She did not believe in signs, but on the other hand she could not stop looking at the spots and remembering her miscarriage, the one before Alexander, the baby, the miscarriage she didn't tell George about, for fear of upsetting him. That was how her pains had started, as red splashes on her yellowing thighs. There followed an agony that threw her onto the bathroom floor. She recalled thinking, as the blood splattered down her legs and she grabbed the rim of the toilet to keep from fainting, that it was good that Daniel, Mark, and Deidre were at school. The consummate mother. She lost a girl. It was not far enough along for it to have mass and definition, but she sensed that it was a girl. She would have named her Catherine, which meant pure, so that the child would not be afflicted by George's moodiness. Catherine. Not big enough yet to have eyes or belly or genuine limbs. Catherine was all blood. The mass of what she was seemed to look at Maria Luisa and cry that she was hungry.

Maria Luisa had cleaned herself up and been able to start dinner when the children came home, and George's searching for work was done for the day. He had not yet settled for his job as a valet at the one good restaurant in town, when they were all of them beyond humiliation. Dinner that night was baked potatoes and canned soup, and she ate George's portion, and also what the children left, and she could not say if it was for herself, or to quiet Catherine.

Just as she could not say if the orchid on the wall recalled for her a similar mighty hunger, or her thighs spread out for husband and children to see.

Cymbidiums may have what is known as a "growing eye," or a growth on the back of the bulb. Leave the eye exposed, in the air;

when it's healthy and ready (use your instincts to determine when this is), cut off the eye, and it can be regrown.

George could swear the thing was starting to look right at him. It made him uneasy, but also intrigued. He was not getting much sleep waiting for this guy to show up, but sleep ambushed him when he least expected it, and until then, no sense in worrying. Maria Luisa was not interfering. She was firmly in the habit of leaving him alone, not even touching him. Frankly, it was a surprise they'd even had Alexander.

When Daniel came downstairs in his pajamas, George said, Turn right around and march up to bed, kiddo.

No, Daddy. I'm going to watch with you.

You're going to go right upstairs to bed.

Mama said I could stay with you if I wanted. She said the orchids were helping me.

Mama is a permissive hippie, I see. Let the kids do whatever they want, and they'll muddle through.

She's a what?

Nothing. A hippie is a kind of person we all were when we thought everything would turn out fine just because we wished it that way.

Oh. I thought Mama was from Portugal, said Daniel, not sure what his father was talking about.

She was. She came here because when we were younger California was a terrific place to be a hippie. Never mind about us. Let's chat about you, buddy. Exactly how are the orchids helping you?

Got me. Sister Angela says they are.

And are they?

I drew some big bear hands holding one.

I see. That's very impressive. How is that a help, do you think, buddy?

Daniel sighed heavily, to indicate that he only wanted to be next to him and not have to cut open whatever they said. He lifted a corner of the blanket covering his father and scooted underneath. His father was warm.

George put his arm around him and leaned back against the paneling on the wall. Maria Luisa and the teacher called them monster hands, but Daniel said they were bear's hands. George could scarcely figure what to call things himself, much less how to mend them. What could he call reaching out his arm that one time and having it bloom into a ragged mess from a bullet that proceeded to explode in his comrade? His arm was growing much older than the rest of him, the hair on it already prematurely white. He hadn't known that parts of the same person might age differently. He could see that but not fix it, just as he could see that Daniel was drawing some symbol of his father's grief: detached hands, because they wanted to get away from the white-haired arm.

Tell me what you think your bear's hands were doing holding an orchid, George said.

Oh, Daddy. Daniel straightened his legs with a thump under the blanket. They're hands. It was a flower. Can't a flower just be a flower?

I wish that were true. But until God chooses to speak to us directly, I'm afraid we have to ask ourselves what things stand for. I'm sorry about this being the rule, but I didn't invent it.

Daniel breathed gently. His father was sounding crazy again. He was mad at himself for telling his mother about that stupid drawing anyway, and at Sister Angela for saying it was good. It sounded like his dad was going to hell for questioning God's rules. Not that Daniel was sure he believed in God. There, he'd thought it out loud inside his head. Now he was going to hell, like his dad. Mother and Deidre and Mark and Alexander would probably go to heaven and have to send them food.

Let's go to sleep, Daddy.

I don't sleep very well. Besides, I need to catch this man. I want to talk to him.

Oh, right, said Daniel, shutting his eyes.

George brushed a mosquito away from Daniel's head. Maybe Daniel was right. The orchid was an orchid, and may it rest in peace as an orchid.

But why did those orchids on the wall not smell good? That

was what he was going to ask the orchid man, when he trapped him. They smelled like a poisonous gas, actually. One sniff could ruin a man's appetite. Hideous. Everything was conspiring to take the taste of things away from him. Why did Maria Luisa insist on making those eggs in bread that looked as if it had been shot through the middle, with the egg oozing like stuff out of a wound—he was going to be sick just thinking about it.

He shouldn't blame her. A man who has seen hunger—which has a smell, an overwhelming odor that seeps over the ground— he smells hunger everywhere after that. It takes shape and hangs in the air, hunger, it smells like a mouth that hasn't eaten in a long time, and out of the mouth the smell of hunger billows, from the far curving edges of the globe. Knowing what hunger was like would have to come to everyone, before everyone could understand the world.

One popular potting medium is osmunda. *This can be made at home, by chopping the roots of tree ferns into a mulch. Commercial mixes are also available,* but Afonso preferred to create his own, in order to limit his trips to gardening centers. All of them, from Lodi to Modesto, were filled with young girls wearing aprons asking if he needed their help.

He packed some loose root ends of decaying ferns into a plastic container. In a week or so, they would be a mossy black. Some of the orchids needed extra nutrients, like the ones in MacMillan's drafty garage, but he was afraid of that cop coming after him, especially if he thought another man was leaving him a corsage. Afonso laughed.

He saw himself standing near the wall of the Castle of São Jorge, with the whole of Lisbon at his feet, as he promised Leonor he would finish his stint in the army and come back to marry her. One of the white peacocks that lived on the castle's grounds strolled near them, pecking.

They had laughed and thrown cracked seed at the white bird.

He had not planned on seeing the soul blister and leave the eyes of that African girl. He did not call Leonor when he returned. She was too young for him to behold, and he could not look at

Lisbon either, since it had been in its presence that he had made a promise to Leonor that he could not keep.

He carried the osmunda, a planting tool, and a filled watering can outside. The night was a black stole, and drying grasses along the roadside confused themselves into a single fragrance of fox-tails. The water was heavy, but the orchids at the Sousa place might need it. He set down the can and fastened the top button of his coat. It was cold, and he had a sensation that he was being watched. Someone was following him, and that made him unbearably sad, that even with a mission like this there could be no peace.

At the Sousa's house, he was unnerved to find the door open. Too easy. That always meant a trap. A rod of moonlight made by the cracked door sliced him in half as he entered the downstairs room. He saw eyes glowing. His instincts were failing him, not to have felt someone lying in wait! As the crouched figure moved forward, Afonso reached out to pull the door shut, but a voice called out, Shh. Wait. I've been waiting for you. Don't be afraid.

Afonso opened the door again. You've what?

Been waiting. Come in, but keep your voice down. My boy Daniel is sleeping.

I'm not asleep, Daddy. Who is it?

Hello, Daniel. I won't hurt you, said Afonso quickly.

You're the orchid man, said George. Afonso Ramires, isn't it? I recognized you in the hardware store.

How did you know?

I know these things.

Afonso had warned himself that at some point someone would find him out. It was a relief. But he didn't know how to explain himself. The way he had matters worked out in his head sounded insane if they were spoken.

I didn't mean to bother you, Afonso whispered.

You didn't, Daniel spoke up. He recalled wanting to tell the man thank you, and that he'd recognized him in the hardware store as well. But then he would probably have to say why he was thanking him, since adults always asked for reasons even though they never offered any themselves. The man was looking at his father. Daniel wasn't as courageous as he thought he would be with this stranger. Not being brave was a terrible thing to find out. It made him a little angry with the orchid man.

I need to know why, that's all, said George.

Why? said Afonso.

See? thought Daniel. Explain this, explain that, explain yourself.

Why plant orchids or anything, said George. Let me help you. I know you were a soldier, and don't ask me how I know because I'm guessing on account of how you move acting like you don't know where's safe to touch. From your accent I have a good idea where you got shipped.

You do? Afonso was startled.

Of course. My wife is from Portugal too, and so were my parents. I was born in Manteca, myself. The Luso-American community there is reasonably big. A few of the people there might be suffering the way you are. I might be, if my parents had stayed overseas. But I was a young American man in the late sixties, and I was sent to—

I know where you were, said Afonso. I can spot a soldier in the dark myself.

Can you? said George. Funny how it's all variations on the same war theme.

Daniel was very excited. There was no fear coming off his father, none. He changed his mind about wanting to thank the man, and instead hoped this would be an adventure. This might end up a good story to tell his friends, with his father capturing the enemy and making him talk.

Wars get fought the same now, said Afonso. It's going off to tie a place into a neat bow, and instead it gets knotted and knotted.

Shh. My wife and kids are sleeping upstairs, said George.

Knotted and knotted, said Afonso. He inhaled sharply. George Sousa might be able to hear what he had to say and not laugh. They were both knotted up. He pointed to the orchids on the bark slabs and said, Those are come to think of it my way of putting up nice clean bows again. Make people at ease.

Have you smelled those things? asked George.

Daniel tensed. Talking about knots reminded him of what he had learned in Scouts, and he was ready to help his father tie this strange person up. Why wasn't his father capturing this man?

Smelled them? asked Afonso. He stepped over to the corner where the orchids shimmered in the dark room. He inhaled again; his face wrinkled horribly. He had picked *Castasetum macrocarpum* because they were hardy, and because whenever an insect landed on them, they shot pollen at it to protect themselves. They didn't smell very pleasant, that was true. He had never noticed this.

But they're beautiful, aren't they? Afonso asked.

Daniel looked anxiously at his father. Weren't they? Why was his father's arm trembling?

Beautiful? With those red splatters? said George.

Red splatters? Red splatters? Afonso was going to strangle on his words. He closed his eyes but that only forced him to stare more closely at the pictures of the African girl flaring in his head. It was regrettable business, this setting out to do a kindness, when the world saw it every which way! Grotesque business! He hated symbols, with a sudden full hatred; he wanted to say he was sorry about what he had done in the past, here were some corsages, and that was that. He wanted to hang up decorations, the end. They were not supposed to be dripping with blood.

Oh, hell. Oh, God, said Afonso. I'll take them down.

No! said Daniel. But the men weren't listening to him. This was stupid. Wasn't his father going to grab this guy's ankles? Then Daniel could run into the garage and come back with a rope.

Sit down, said George. You know how Freud says the unconscious can't tell the difference between a real memory and an invented one? What're the chances that you and I fell into a dream and that's all?

Not good. We invent explanations, after the fact. We can't say what our actions are until after we've done them, if then, said Afonso.

I know. I know, said George. I was trying to put a nice face on what happened to us, saying it might be dreamed up.

Nice face, thought Afonso. Everything got personified; petals could be a girl.

Who was Freud? wondered Daniel. This was dumb! Where was the fight? How could his father be a hero without a fight?

Want something to drink? asked George.

I'd better be going. I'd wager I was followed, said Afonso. There's someone out there after me.

Come back tomorrow night. I'm pleased to meet another man who doesn't sleep. You come back and I'll pour you a drink, and if someone's following you we'll outrun him.

Me too, thought Daniel. Me too. This was more like it.

Careful of leaf scorch! Orchid leaves can get black-tipped if the light is too strong.

Maria Luisa felt javelins of morning sunlight coming through the window, hitting her in the head. Once again George was not beside her. She picked at a loose thread in the blanket, sat up, and decided she was tired of savoring her time alone. There had been another man's voice downstairs, she was sure of it, and she was going to call the police and tell Officer MacMillan to keep an eye on their house. It was just like George, or rather the George she was living with now, to invite a stranger in, and no telling what that could lead to.

It was time to end this oddball gardening, especially with Daniel involved.

She got out of bed and put on her robe. It always felt as if her job consisted of attaching the morning to some cable that would allow the day to glide on like a streetcar. What would happen, if she did nothing but give that streetcar a push and wish it good luck? Alexander was crying down the hall. Heading toward him, she thought it was really too bad that the stranger had not intended the flowers for her.

John Lindley (1799–1865), an acknowledged expert on orchids, named more than 3,000 species. H. G. Reichenbach (1823–1889) was responsible for naming even more. The current estimate of the number of species ranges from 15,000 to 30,000, a staggering number that is in some ways most impressive on account of the wideness of the range. *The normal classifications of genus, subtribe, tribe, sub-family, and family are strained to the breaking point.*

He's coming, Daddy. I can hear him.

You can? Your hearing is getting very impressive, Daniel.

Thank you, Daddy. Are we going to tackle him?

No, I don't think so. He seems like a nice man.

Daniel tried to hide his disappointment. He sat still. It crossed his mind that this Afonso and his father could meet in a café if they wanted to talk, that it didn't have to be in the middle of the night like this. Unless they were both desperadoes. This cheered him up.

Afonso was sweating when he knocked on the rec room door. Daniel ran to open it, and right away, from looking at the man's face, he figured something was wrong.

I was followed, I'm sure of it now, said Afonso. He was holding his coat tightly around himself.

Daniel glanced around Afonso, to the outside. The wind was blowing and there was nothing except the heavier stain of darkness that distinguished the ground from the air. The orchids high on their bark slabs shook a little.

George marveled at how serene it seemed, and yet he too, like Afonso, sensed that someone was out there. It wasn't frightening. It was only someone who wanted to chase them, and past the clearness of the fields were the hills with their firs, looming like a shelter. George had not truly outwitted another man in quite a while, and there was something to be said for staying in training for that. It was a godsend! To get him off the floor of his rec room and into the open.

We shouldn't sit here like ducks waiting to be shot on a pond, said George.

Let's go, then, said Afonso. Where?

Daniel was putting on his tennis shoes, his heart beating fast. He knew how every boring day ended, but not this one; finally here was one he couldn't predict the outcome of.

The heads of all three of them snapped up as they heard a gunshot crack into the clear glass of the night.

Jesus! said Afonso.

Christ Almighty, said George. What'd you do?

Nothing! I swear it, said Afonso. Put up orchids. That's it.

Maybe they've gone and passed some wacko new ordinance, said George. You know our city council. In any case I think we should lead them away from the house. I got kids upstairs.

Sanctuary! Daniel almost screamed, too excited to contain himself. Sanctuary!

You're going up those stairs, said George. Go on.

I have to take you to sanctuary! said Daniel.

Upstairs.

Sanctuary! Sister Angela says that in the old days no matter what a guy did, he could go into a holy place like a church and no one could get him there. Everybody agreed it wasn't allowed.

I don't think people nowadays honor that idea, Daniel, said Afonso.

Sister Angela will make them! said Daniel. She'll make them! She tells me that she leaves her window unlocked so that if I ever need anything or get in trouble I should come to her. No matter what. She has a guitar in her room and said she would teach me some chords.

The sound of another gunshot echoed.

George was trembling. Gunfire? Over orchids? What was this?

Daniel. Go on. Now, said George.

Daddy! Come on! Daniel knew his father would make him go upstairs unless he acted fast. If he ran out the door, his father and the orchid man would have to follow him, if only to capture him and send him to his room. He dashed through the door, with his father and his father's friend running after him. Daniel took deep breaths and kept his head low, the way he had seen them do in movies, as he rushed across the field. The convent was over a mile away, and the men were gaining on him. His father used to be a good runner, but he had lost a lot of weight, and he couldn't swing his arms. It was too bad that there were no more gunshots. It could be that the gunman understood about sanctuary and was waiting for them at the convent. Daniel began to feel sick from running so hard, but when the convent was in sight, he slowed down, his legs cramping. His father caught him, but now that they were almost to the end of where they were heading, he wasn't going to send him home.

Daniel threw some pebbles at Sister Angela's window. She often stayed in her room reading at night, she had told the class. She liked to improve her mind. God approved of that kind of thing.

Sister! Daniel shouted.

She came without her veil to the window. When she saw Daniel and the men outside, she put on her wimple and veil and leaned out the window to talk to them. Daniel was breathless, and his father had to explain that they were running away because someone they couldn't see was chasing them, and there was a gun involved.

That was all Sister Angela needed to hear. She waved them around to the front of the Mount Carmel Convent.

Shh, she said, unlocking the door for them. She wanted so much to see a vision. She tried not to hope for one too much, because desiring it could scare it away. Surprises that involved mortals, like this one, would have to substitute in the meantime for a more sublime visitation. Besides, she was peeved at the other nuns for putting more locks on the door. Why this need to keep the world out? Let it in! Let it barge in!

Gosh, giggled Sister Angela as the men went to sit with her in the chapel. This is great. I feel as if I'm in *The Sound of Music*.

Keep him here, said George. We're going to go find out what's happening.

Daddy, said Daniel.

Afonso was on his feet too.

I'll watch him, said Sister Angela. When will you come back?

When we find out what's happening, said George.

I'm going with you! said Daniel.

No, said Sister Angela. You and I are going to the commissary for some chocolate.

No, I'm not.

If there are—Sister Angela wanted to say to George and this other man that since a gun was involved, they should call for help.

The police—Sister Angela held onto Daniel's arm as he squirmed.

It might be the police we're trying to avoid, said Afonso. I planted these orchids, see, and that's breaking and entering, I suppose. But I don't think that requires gunfire.

No, I certainly agree, said Sister Angela. Those orchids were a gift, sir, and I thank you.

Afonso thought of saying "you're welcome," but those orchids had turned into so much trouble he was forgetting normal manners.

Me too. Thanks, said Daniel.

George leaned down to kiss the top of his son's head. He explained to Daniel that sanctuary was a perfect place to be, and that anyhow they needed someone in command central, in case they had to send messages. Sister Angela mentioned again that they would have chocolate.

As George and Afonso left the convent, Daniel realized his mistake. He had been bribed by food, and his father was now out at war.

Strangely enough, orchid bulbs are fruitful, but seeds alone do not germinate readily in nature. A certain fungal infection that seeps into the roots is required, to assist in metabolism. (Cultures may be started with an agar solution in a glass flask.) The fungus remains for the entire life of the plant. You might say everything needs its hidden itch.

Whadja do such an asinine thing for? The man planted orchids, and as far as I can see that's no capital offense, said Bettencourt.

I wasn't aiming at anyone! I was shooting at some goddamn birds, you saw me! said MacMillan. Here in Lodi there ain't much cause to pull a gun, and my hand was craving the sound of it, that's all. Come to think of it I don't give a shit about some oar-kids.

I'm a fool for agreeing to ride with you, said Bettencourt. You've got about ten screws loose. I didn't want anybody breaking onto my ranch, just wanted to scare him some, but now I don't care much what he does.

MacMillan shivered. If only this orchid stuff hadn't happened during a time when he felt so constantly hungry. When men got hungry, there was no accounting for anything they did. Bettencourt, hell, with the way he slaughtered his steers and had his way with whatever and whomever he wanted, what would he know about feeling like there wasn't enough food in the world to satisfy a gut, which in every man was no bigger than the size of a bunched fist?

Orchids, unlike all other flowers, have a single reproductive structure, which is why they have those distinctive columns in their centers. These are made up of a fusion of stamen and pistil.

Wars are fought in forests now, said George. You notice that?

No more lining up in red coats and firing at rows of soldiers, that's right, said Afonso. It had been awhile since he had run so hard and fast, and the earth was spinning and making him see red spots. The vegetation high in the trees of the thin forest looked like small bursts of flak. How had everything come to this?

I'm turning in for the night, myself, said George.

Better climb into the trees.

Mountain lions can climb.

I know it. We'll have to take our chances. I want to sleep on a bough because men are chasing us and they usually forget to look upward.

You've got a point.

As they paused a moment on the ground, George wiped his sweating face with his sleeve. His Swiss knife was in his pocket, and he took it out to clean his nails. He cleaned his hands every night before bed, no matter where he was, so that the white-haired arm would not make them old. Crickets sang low and steadily as he clipped his fingernails.

To his astonishment, and as Afonso watched dumbfounded, the parings of nail jumped together into an ill-defined little horny animal. It used its sharp edges to rip through the grass and escape. It wheeled onward, jerkily.

Good-bye, you drained modern creatures, called out the creature made of George's nails. I must go out to search for God.

Good-bye, said George. What else was there to say? It made sense that even the discarded parts of him would yearn for the pursuit of someone who might know the grand plan.

Now I damn well know I want to sleep off the ground, said Afonso.

They both climbed up, into separate trees.

From his limb, George tried to spy on the creature made of his nails going out on its search, but that was impossible. It was receding. O well; there was nothing to do about that but wish it luck. He was not afraid of falling; he might as well be rooted to this tree forever. That was how light and secure he felt now. What was a body, in the end, but thin tissue and bits of shading?

Afonso slapped at a gnat. He was going to wake up covered with red spots, at this rate. He dozed and thought of the razor-sharp animal of nails spiking through the open fields, and he asked his soul to follow it. To follow it, to fly away, to Africa. He might be able to undo what was done. He might be able to undo, also, what he had left undone.

He peered in the dark to see his comrade. Where had he climbed? Into one of those trees over there. But instead of spotting George, Afonso, clinging to his branch, detected orchids growing high on a tree. There were other orchids in other trees. He was surrounded by them, by the eyes of the girl. During his escapade of presenting corsages to Lodi, had he planted the flowers here too, to remake the forest, and forgotten about that? Was that possible?

Your soul cannot go anew to Africa, his body spoke to him. It is already there, where you left it.

Orchids need not be a mystery. Consider that they thrive in conditions that most humans want: Keep them dry and fed; lighted, but not exposed to too much heat; give them peace and quiet; allow for ventilation; do not expect a constant bloom.

On that trip to Lisbon, after the wound in George's arm healed, Maria Luisa drove them north to Conimbriga, where mosaics from the ruins of a Roman settlement covered the ground. A Minotaur guarded the center of a labyrinth in the museum, which the sign said might have been a game constructed for the entertainment of the family that once lived on that site. Some olive trees, which could take care of themselves, stood near the perimeter of the ruins, while some scraggly rose trees gave testimony to lack of upkeep. The Romans had not survived there long, before Franks and Almans and Swabians invaded.

Maria Luisa could picture the shrieking children playing in the labyrinth, but was the point to find the Minotaur or avoid it? In any case that was how it went with families: set up a twisting path, trap the monster, run about. That was how the Lusitanian mind worked, too—in mosaics. As if it said, Please put the glorious big pictures in small blocks, so that we can manage the lushness of what they are without being overwhelmed.

She put on her *fado* record for the third time that day. There were a number of merry *fados*, but she did not care so much for those. Let the *fadistas* sing of their travails, let them weep for her. If she cried herself, it might frighten the children.

On her desk was the drawing Daniel had done in class that day. There were no hands or orchids; only a blank.

Why, honey? she had said. What is it?

Air, he had said. The thing that orchids eat to live. My father is lost inside it, and I have to wait until it speaks to me.

ACKNOWLEDGMENTS

I would like to thank the National Endowment for the Arts for their support. I also wish to acknowledge Oakley Hall, founder and previous director of the program in writing at the University of California, Irvine, and the late MacDonald Harris. Thanks as well to Barbara Hall and Ann Heiney.

Several stories, some in different forms, were originally published in various publications and are reprinted here with permission: *The American Voice* ("Still Life"); *Black Ice* ("Original Sin"); *Nimrod* ("Island Fever"); *Other Voices* ("Add Blue to Make White Whiter"); *Spunk, an International Journal of the Arts* ("The Birth of Water Stories"); and *Triquarterly* ("Fado").

Both "Original Sin" and "Fado" were the first inspirations for my novel *Saudade* (New York: St. Martin's Press, 1994), and traces of both may be found there.

The epigraph on page vii is from the sonnet "?" by Florbela Espanca, in *Sonetos*, compiled by José Régio, p. 149 (Amadora, Portugal: Livraria Bertrand, SARL, Apartado 37, 1980, 20th ed.). The translation is mine.

The epigraph for "My Hunt for King Sebastião" is from "Third," in the cycle "Warnings," in *Mensagem* (Message), by Fernando Pessoa, translated by Jonathan Griffin, pp. 92–93 (London: Menard Press, King's College, 1992). Reprinted with permission.

I gratefully acknowledge several volumes that were useful in my research: For "Undressing the Vanity Dolls," *The Language of Flowers* (anonymous, but compiled by Margaret Pickston (England: Michael Joseph Ltd., 1968; distributed in the United States by The Yeoman Group, New York). For "The Remains of Princess Kaiulani's Garden," *Women of Old Hawaii,* by Maxine Mrantz (Honolulu: Aloha Publishing, 1975); *Hawaii's Tragic Princess,* by Maxine Mrantz (Honolulu: Aloha Publishing, 1980); and *Stolen Kingdom,* by Rich Budnick, with an introduction by Governor John Waihee (Honolulu: Aloha Press, 1992). For "How to Grow Orchids Without Grounds: A Manual," *Orchids for the Home & Greenhouse,* Barbara B. Pesch, director of publications (Brooklyn, N.Y.: Brooklyn Botanic Garden Record, 1990); and *Orchids,* Kathryn L. Arthurs, supervising editor (Menlo Park, Calif.: Sunset Publishing, 1970, 1977).

Though it is true that the Portuguese brought the *braguinha* to Hawaii and it became known as the ukulele, and the members of the Hawaiian royal family who are mentioned did exist and the related historical events and legends occurred, the Portuguese characters in "The Remains of Princess Kaiulani's Garden" are fictional, as is the story itself. Readers may consult any comprehensive book about Hawaiian music for the historical facts concerning the various Portuguese immigrants first linked to the playing or constructing of the ukulele and regarding the various audiences with King Kalakaua, but any similarities between them and my characters are coincidental.

PREVIOUS WINNERS OF THE

DRUE HEINZ LITERATURE PRIZE

The Death of Decartes, David Bosworth, 1981

Dancing for Men, Robley Wilson, 1982

Private Parties, Jonathan Penner, 1983

The Luckiest Man in the World, Randall Silvis, 1984

The Man Who Loved Levittown, W. D. Wetherell, 1985

Under the Wheat, Rick De Marinis, 1986

In the Music Library, Ellen Hunnicutt, 1987

Moustapha's Eclipse, Reginald McKnight, 1988

Cartographies, Maya Sonenberg, 1989

Limbo River, Rick Hillis, 1990

Have You Seen Me?, Elizabeth Graver, 1991

Director of the World and Other Stories, Jane McCafferty, 1992

In the Walled City, Stewart O'Nan, 1993

Departures, Jennifer C. Cornell, 1994

Dangerous Men, Geoffrey Becker, 1995

Vaquita and Other Stories, Edith Pearlman, 1996